MAY

MAY

The Hard-Rock Life of Pioneer
May Arkwright Hutton

MARY BARMEYER O'BRIEN

TWODOT®

Guilford, Connecticut
Helena, Montana
An imprint of Globe Pequot Press

Very Good

A · TWODOT® · BOOK

Map by Mapping Specialists Ltd. © Morris Book Publishing, LLC

Project editor: Meredith Dias
Layout: Sue Murray

Library of Congress Cataloging-in-Publication Data

O'Brien, Mary Barmeyer.
  May : the hard-rock life of pioneer May Arkwright Hutton·/ Mary
Barmeyer O'Brien.
    pages cm
  ISBN 978-0-7627-7345-9
  1. Hutton, May Arkwright—Fiction. 2. Women pioneers—Fiction. 3.
Suffragists—Fiction. 4. Biographical fiction. I. Title.
  PS3615.B76M39 2013
  813'.6—dc23
                        2012050337

Printed in the United States of America

10 9 8 7 6 5 4 3 2 1

This is a work of fiction. Although the account is based on May Arkwright Hutton's life, some of the events, characters, circumstances, names, points in time, places, and details are imagined or have been slightly modified to fit the story.

TO THE CHILDREN AND STAFF
OF THE
HUTTON SETTLEMENT

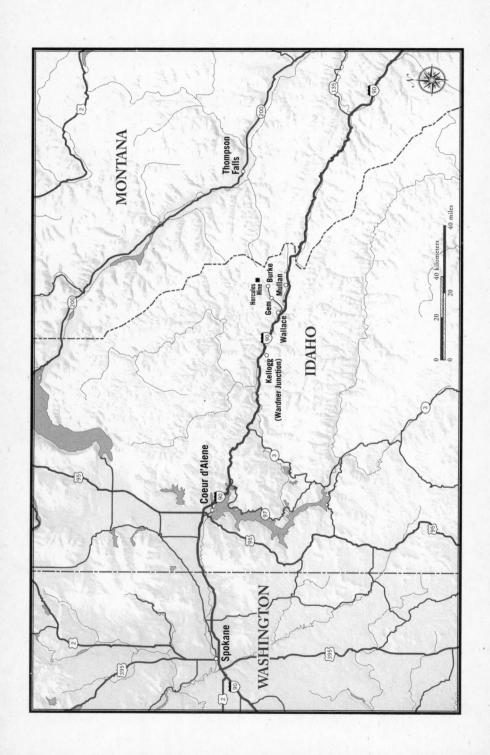

MONTANA

Thompson
Falls

Burke
Hercules
Mine
Gem Mullan
Wallace

Kellogg
(Wardner Junction)

IDAHO

Coeur d'Alene

Spokane

WASHINGTON

0   20   40 kilometers
0   20   40 miles

PART I
1883–1892

CHAPTER 1

Summer 1883

THESE MOUNTAINS COULD MAKE A WOMAN RICH. THEY JUTTED STRAIGHT up to heaven, so steep and magnificent that May Arkwright had to hold on to her flowered hat and tip her head back to see the tops. The way they towered above her and stabbed into the deep blue sky took her breath away. There was nothing like them back in Ohio, where the tame countryside barely rippled with low hills. Here in northern Idaho Territory, the dark green vertical slopes had a glorious presence that made a woman feel as if they really did hold the treasures advertised in the flyer tucked safely in her bodice.

She hoped the little town of Eagle City was in the narrow canyon up ahead and not perched high on these forested cliffs. The dusty black pony beneath her was sturdy, but not sturdy enough to haul her up any mountainsides. She couldn't imagine living in a place where the earth dropped off right under your feet. After twenty-three years of growing up on flat Ohio streets, nothing would be more unsettling.

She'd best stop gawking and get riding. May brushed off her rumpled blue skirt and tucked her scuffed boots tighter into the stirrups. Sweat trickled down her round face; she swiped at it with a dirty driving glove and stuffed a loose wisp of brown hair under her hat. The men were out of sight now, except for Jim Wardner, who dutifully stopped and waited for her every mile or so.

"Hurry up a bit, can't you, Miss Arkwright?" Wardner fretted as he guided his horse closer. "I don't like the feel of that breeze. It's blowing in a mountain thunderstorm, and you'll want to be situated when it hits. Summer storms come up fast here. You can't see far enough to know they're brewing."

"You hurry on ahead, Jim. This poor pony can't do much better with me weighing him down, and I'm not afraid of a little thunder and rain. A bit of rain never hurt anybody."

"Well, it's more likely to be a downpour. And I'm not about to leave you alone. An unescorted lady would be a novelty in Eagle City, believe me. Kick that little chap in the ribs and let's get moving."

May gingerly touched the pony's sides with her heels, and he broke into a labored trot. She clutched her big wicker basket to her side and tried to keep her belongings from jostling out. Wouldn't that be a sight! Littering the road behind her with corsets and stockings and knee-length drawers. She probably should have bought a valise like other women, but it seemed a shame to spend her hard-earned money on a carry case and let this good sturdy basket go to waste. Her necessities fit inside, even if they were in disarray. It didn't matter if her personal things were exposed for the world to see. Who hadn't already been privy to the sight of a woman's corset?

Damn, she was sore from all this riding. Her backside was rubbed raw from the saddle, and trotting wasn't helping matters. She pulled on the reins, and the pony dropped again to a walk. Jim could go ahead if he wanted to beat the rain. Even though she was glad for his advice, he needn't think he could boss May Arkwright around. She hadn't come all this way to be told by a man what to do. But Jim just pulled on his own reins and plodded beside her.

So far, her decision to come west seemed like a good one. She'd find her fortune out here if it killed her. In the meantime, she could be as independent and improper as she wanted. Western mining towns were so rough and bawdy that no one batted an eyelash if you were unconventional. Maybe she'd fit in better here than back home. And she sure as hell didn't want to be stuck in the Midwest all her life watching the corn grow, when opportunity out here waited for those bold enough to grab it. By now, she knew exactly what gold fever was. She had a whopping case of it herself.

She had to admit, though, that there had been a tiny knot of uneasiness in the pit of her stomach ever since they'd left the boat at Lake Coeur d'Alene and begun the last leg of the journey on horseback. But, heck, what woman wouldn't be a little nervous? Here she was, two thousand miles from home, riding through wilderness so dense that, except for the two meandering wagon tracks her pony followed, it seemed as if nobody had been here before. She took a deep breath and pushed her worries away. No need to dwell on thoughts of surviving the icy winter, and the dwindling number of coins in her purse.

Maybe she should give her poor pony a rest. That wouldn't get her to Eagle City in time, though. The forty men she'd traveled with from the Midwest would be scattered to the hills by then; they were that eager to begin staking their claims. May wanted to send them off with hearty good-byes and good wishes for a lucky find. Some of those fellows felt like brothers now that they had traveled so far together. She had been the only woman in the group, and they'd treated her just fine.

The dirt tracks disappeared into the canyon. It seemed as though the twisting trail would never end. She shifted irritably in the saddle. Riding a pony was a lot harder than it looked.

Just when she felt she couldn't endure another step, they rounded a corner and spotted fresh gashes on the slopes and piles of reddish tailings spilling toward a handful of dilapidated shacks below.

"That's not Eagle City, is it, Jim? Those shacks up ahead?" A few rough buildings with false fronts were squeezed close to the mountains on the banks of a bubbling creek that flowed down the center of the gulch. There was a cluster of lopsided cabins that looked as if they'd been thrown together from unpeeled logs. Off to one side were some sagging gray tents. If this was the "town" Jim had described when she'd met him on the train, she wondered about the restaurant where he'd asked her to cook. As they had hurtled west, he'd told her that he was searching for a woman to feed the miners in the boomtown of Eagle City. He had a shipping business there and knew the men wanted something besides their own bad grub.

Heck, she could cook anywhere there was a stove. It would be a fine way to get started in her new life. But it would be nice if there were a place to sleep, too, and a privy not far from the back door.

"Yep, that's her all right." Jim's deep voice sang out. "That's the residential district up there. I'll take you to the saloon where the restaurant is. That wind's picking up."

May scanned the mining camp again and then turned her eyes to the foothills. A few shacks climbed the slope, scattered among piles of dirt, trash, and machinery. Their sagging doorways and dreary walls faced her. The ground was raw dirt. One hard-packed, rutted street slashed the town in half. A couple of scruffy men leaned on shovels and watched her curiously. May swallowed, sat up straighter, and drew her shoulders back.

Jim glanced at her. His coat had dust in the creases, and his face looked weary after the long ride. His long brown mustache blew in the breeze, hiding what looked to May like a small grin.

"The restaurant isn't a palace, Miss Arkwright," he said, as if he knew what she was thinking. "It's pretty small. The pack rats aren't bad, though. Just watch the stove so you don't set the roof on fire. 'Course, most the time the roof is covered with snow. It doesn't leak much, only in the spring during the melt—and when there's a gully washer."

May gazed across at him and lifted her chin.

"I can cook under a leaky roof, Jim. And just wait until I get my hands on a pack rat or two." She winked. "Maybe they'd be good in a nice hot stew."

CHAPTER 2

Summer 1883

MAY OPENED HER EYES IN THE DARKNESS AND PULLED THE SCRATCHY wool blanket to her chin. Damn, was she cold! The nights at this altitude didn't stay warm like they did back home. She buried her face under the blanket but immediately felt as though she were suffocating, so she poked her nose out again. Wriggling onto her side, she tried to get comfortable. This so-called bed—just a couple of planks nailed to the shanty's walls— was as hard as the rusty iron cookstove on the other side of the wall. It didn't help that her whole body ached from the two-day pony ride.

She turned over again, but the planks pressed into her shoulder and hip. With a sigh, she sat up, leaned against the splintery walls, and pulled the blanket up around her neck. Moonlight poured through the vertical cracks in the wall and made stripes across the dirt floor. Something rustled in the corner where her basket was stowed. May peered into the darkness. Heck, it was probably just a mouse, but Jim's comment about pack rats bothered her. She wasn't squeamish. Rats, though, weren't her favorite of God's creatures. Why He created a bold, beady-eyed rodent that gnawed on people's good boots and apron strings was a mystery to her. They smelled bad, too. The musky stench rose from every corner of the shack.

She leaned over and plucked her basket from the floor. There was a loud squeak, more rustling, and then silence. May guessed the animal had squeezed through the nearest crack to the outside. She put the basket on the foot of her bed anyway.

Despite her fatigue, she didn't feel sleepy. She rose and, trailing the blanket, stepped into the main room. Her apartment, as Jim had called it, was just a lean-to abutting the back of the rough structure that was his restaurant. The main room was warmer, since the stove still held some heat from the supper she had fixed for herself. She stood for a moment in the curtained doorway and studied the lopsided stove and the moonlight pouring in a small square in the door, where someone with lofty ideas about glass windows had cut a hole. Then she crossed the room, the dirt floor cold on her bare feet, and looked outside. The mining camp lay silent, bathed in silvery moonlight that silhouetted the mountains and the jagged tips of the pines. A creek burbled quietly through the clearing.

A shiver of excitement ran through her. She'd done it! Despite everyone's warnings, she had come west. Her half-brother Lyman had pointed out every danger and impropriety, including the fact that there would be no place to live when she arrived, and no chaperone. But, heck, she could take care of herself, and quite capably, too. Hundreds of women came out here without the proper gentlemen to accompany them. Most of them were red-light girls, but that didn't mean a hardworking cook like herself couldn't do it—and maybe get rich at the same time. She would earn an honest living but also keep an ear cocked for news of lucky gold or silver strikes. Maybe she could buy interests in a few diggings, or try panning for gold herself. Why couldn't a person just use a pie pan instead of one of those expensive gold pans?

When she was rich someday, she'd have the means to change the world. She hadn't spent her childhood listening to political speakers for nothing. For years, she had led her blind grandfather by the hand to the town square so he could listen to every orator, politician, and preacher who traveled through—and formed her own strong opinions about how the world should be. It was time to change a few things, that was for sure.

May pulled the blanket tighter and tugged open the creaky door. It dragged across the dirt, sagging on its metal hinges. She stepped into the night air. Only the brightest stars twinkled through the moonlight. Every tree and blade of grass cast a distinct shadow.

She'd seen enough misery and wrongdoing in her life to have some big dreams. Children who had lost both parents grabbed her heartstrings the most. She herself had been lucky enough to have Granddad, but there were plenty of other little tykes cast out into the world alone.

And then there were America's women, who, in her opinion, were treated like second-class citizens. They weren't even allowed to vote. She didn't want to start thinking about it at this hour. It would get her so riled up she'd never go back to sleep.

She took a deep breath of mountain air and went inside, forcing the door shut behind her. A star twinkled at her through the hole where the stovepipe shoved up through the flimsy roof. May pushed the curtain aside and lay down on the hard planks again. Tomorrow would come too soon, and with it her first customers. She'd better be rested and ready to cook up a big, tasty breakfast for them.

It was a humble beginning here in Idaho Territory. This shed left a lot to be desired. But it was a start. She could leave the past behind and never mention it again if she wanted. Goodness knew she didn't want to advertise that she had been born to parents who both deserted her when she was only ten, or that she had already been married twice.

She didn't want to think about those marriages, much less talk about them. As far as she was concerned, they were in the past, and that was that.

Oh, she had a few good memories, especially of Granddad. But now she was on her own. And here she was, deep in the Rocky Mountains far from any real civilization, hell-bent on making her fortune. Then she would light out to change the world.

CHAPTER 3

Early Summer 1887

COOKING IN SOMEONE ELSE'S RESTAURANT—FIRST IN THAT SALOON IN Eagle City and then in nearby Murrayville—had been a jim-dandy way to get settled, but already four years had passed without making her any richer. So May had finagled a change: She had opened her own place in this one-room shanty beside the new rail line at Wardner Junction. A big gray board with the word CAFÉ scrawled across it leaned against the front wall of the weathered building. Now she could take in all the profits, not just a meager wage.

May shoved another log into the old cookstove and took a deep, lingering breath. Wood smoke mingled with the smell of the fresh coffee that was brewing for her early morning customers. Careful not to knock over the pail of milk on the floor beside her, she tied the strings of her red calico apron. Her fingers were stiff with cold, despite the hot blaze. That was Idaho Territory for you. Hotter than heck one day and colder than ice the next. No one would guess it was summer. Cold hands or not, she'd better make sure her flapjack batter was ready.

Anyone with an ounce of smarts could see that the best place for business was down here beside the new tracks that ran near the Bunker Hill and Sullivan mines. Her customers had followed. By now they were so fond of her savory venison stew and generous slices of huckleberry pie that she could move to the moon and they'd tag along. May chuckled. Nothing like decent home cooking to draw men like flies.

She hoped that handsome Al Hutton would spot her sign from his locomotive. There was something about that man. Whenever he showed up for her fluffy flapjacks on these cold mountain mornings, she felt her face flush more than usual. Her breath came in quick little puffs as she called out to greet him. Usually men didn't affect her that way. She could pal around with the best of them, slapping backs and guffawing at their jokes and acting like one of the boys. But with Al it was different. His good-looking face and quiet manners made him stand out from the crowd of crude miners and grubstakers. There was intelligence in his gray eyes, and none of the silent demands that some men telegraphed to women, as if females were put on earth only to please them. None of that. Al seemed to recognize that this was the 1880s, not the Dark Ages.

The first time she'd met him, she remembered to use her manners and greeted him as "Mr. Hutton." Before long, though, she began calling him Al. Why call him "mister" when the two of them were exactly the same age and he had a perfectly good first name?

May doubted that he was interested in her, although she didn't consider herself homely like most folks did. After all, those old European masterpiece artists had always chosen plump women as their models. She was tall, and a bit more than plump, she admitted, but her features and pale complexion were nice. Her straight nose and dark-fringed eyes weren't bad, and she kept her wavy brown hair as clean as she could. Anyone would agree she had flair with clothes. Ruffles, lace, glass jewels, flowers, bright colors—the more the better—defined her attire. More than anything, she loved wearing dresses that trailed shimmering ribbons and hats heavy with artificial fruit or silk roses. A person could fancy up the plainest of dresses with a few cents worth of embellishments from the dry goods store.

In fact, her dresses—the few she had—were like decorations for her crowded living quarters, separated from the cafe by a yellow gingham curtain. They hung from the back wall in a hand-stitched rainbow of flowing colors—magenta, royal blue, gold, serviceable black, and emerald green.

11

Her bed of boards and a hay-stuffed mattress lined one wall, covered with a knitted purple spread. She'd made a shelf at the head of the bed—hammered those nails herself—for her hairbrush, cracked mirror, and kerosene lamp. The big basket she'd used as a valise on the trip west lay in a corner, filled with potatoes, yams, and squash. Her hats hung around the edge of the ceiling, each on a separate nail.

The door banged open and Jim Wardner stepped in.

"Well, Miss Arkwright, I knew I'd find you where the commerce is—Wardner Junction. You've stepped up in the world. I'm right proud of you—you've got a diner of your own. And here beside the new tracks, too."

"Hullo, Jim. It's a little undersized, but it'll do."

Wardner glanced around before dropping into a chair. The plank walls were weathered gray, with an occasional knothole that offered a glimpse of the outdoors. The curtain that separated the stove and eating area from May's living quarters was half pulled back, exposing her personal belongings. One small window let in the early morning light. May had used pieces of brown burlap as curtains, and they hung crookedly over the window frame. A slit of daylight showed under the sagging plank door and a braided rug lay under the solitary table, which was covered with stained red oilcloth. Around the table, four mismatched chairs were interspersed with a few log stumps.

"One table might not be enough," Jim commented.

"It's all I've got. I could squeeze plenty of men around it if I had more chairs."

"I'll see what I can do. In the meantime, how about some of that homemade bread and a couple of fried eggs?"

"It'll have to be flapjacks. I didn't have time to bake bread yesterday."

"Flapjacks will do. Say, did you hear about the discovery in that gulch near Wallace? They say someone found an outcropping of galena yesterday—a sure sign of silver."

May's pancake flapper stopped in midair.

"It's so steep up there they'll have to use mountain goats to get it out, if the rumor is true. Men are saying there's a good streak of it. If it's so, it might draw the interest of outside investors just like the Bunker Hill and Sullivan mines have. I'm going to ride up . . ." The rest of his words were lost in the loud rumble of train cars and the shriek of a whistle. The window rattled in its frame.

May covered her ears, still holding the flapper, as a black locomotive sped by the window. She craned her neck. It was Al Hutton's, all right. "Damn, I didn't think it would be so noisy in here. I know I'm close to the tracks, but..." May uncovered her ears. "Good thing those trains don't run at night or I'd be shootin' out their headlamps to keep 'em quiet. Say, Jim, let me know what you find out about that galena discovery, will you?"

"I will. I'm going to keep my ear to the ground, I can tell you."

"By the way, what do you think of that train engineer, Al Hutton?" May kept her eyes on the flapjacks and tried to make her question sound casual, as if she'd just been reminded by the train's passing.

But Jim's eyes twinkled. "Why do you ask, Miss Arkwright?"

She felt her face flush. "I just want to know who's making all the racket out there, that's all."

"Well, Hutton's a good man—one of the best. He's smart as a whip. Honest and reliable. Pleasant to speak to, and polite, too." Jim winked. "Maybe you'd best flag him down and invite him to breakfast."

CHAPTER 4

Summer 1887

MAY PUSHED ASIDE THE BUSHES, THANKFUL THAT SHE'D WORN HER overalls. People in these parts peered down their noses at a woman who wore pants, but to hell with them. They weren't the ones clambering around these mountains picking berries for pies. By now, a dress would be ripped and dirty, but these sturdy overalls didn't tear or show the dirt on her knees and the huckleberry stains on the front. Her fingers were purple from the juice. The color had crept under her fingernails. She didn't care. Clean hands weren't all they were cracked up to be.

From her vantage point on the steep slope above Wardner, May could look out over the scenic valley and watch the silver South Fork snake its way west toward Lake Coeur d'Alene. The railroad cut a path down the valley's length, along with meandering dirt wagon roads. In the afternoon sunlight, the canyons etched themselves into the surrounding mountains, each promising riches. From here, only the town of Wardner was visible, but May knew that little mining settlements dotted the length of the forty-mile-long valley. To the east, out of sight, was the town of Wallace and, beyond that, the mountain pass that led to Montana Territory.

It would be nice to have a companion today, but the men were too busy working their claims to bother with berry picking. The women she met around these parts didn't cotton to her for some reason. Maybe they shied away from her earthy comments and loud voice, or the way she joshed with their men. Even their dresses were different, although May wasn't about to change her style. Most of the local ladies wore flowing dark dresses with high collars and modest sleeves. May liked flashy colors and occasional low necklines.

The stillness was shattered by that everlasting train whistle. You could hear the thing all the way to Timbuktu the way it echoed off the mountainsides. If she didn't know better, she might have thought Al Hutton blasted it just to disturb the quiet. But the more she got to know him, the more she was sure he'd have a good reason to toot his whistle. That's how he was. She picked another handful of huckleberries to stir into tomorrow's flapjack batter for him.

Just the thought of Al Hutton made her heart beat faster. Why, the man was as good looking as a stage actor. He was tall and slender—but powerfully built from handling that locomotive—with wavy brown hair that fell over his forehead. It was all she could do sometimes not to reach over and brush it aside for him. And his eyes! Those piercing gray eyes could bewitch a woman. When Al fixed them on her, they seemed to penetrate to her very soul. He was as self-assured as a man could get, yet he wasn't cocky. His quiet confidence made him seem more powerful than ten of those loud-mouthed, brawny miners.

Something was crunching through the underbrush. May stood up and hugged her full tin berry pail, ready to drop it and run. There were bears in these mountains—she'd seen plenty of them on her other expeditions—not to mention cougars, wolves, and moose. She peered through the brush and tree trunks as the crunching got louder, half expecting a wild animal to come loping her way.

"Miss Arkwright, I declare. I run into you in the oddest places. Here I am prospecting and I find you halfway up the mountain."

It was Gus Paulsen, a young miner who trudged these slopes looking for a promising show of galena or a gold nugget in the creek beds. He hadn't had much luck, but it wasn't because he hadn't tried. Months of scrambling up gulches and steep mountainsides with his miner's pick were beginning to show on his face. His clear, pale blue eyes were set

15

narrowly above a bushy blond beard, but May could see that his cheeks had hollowed out underneath. He was muscular and tough, and when he took breakfast at May's cafe, he sat on the edge of his chair as if he could hardly stop long enough to eat. After wolfing down his breakfast and wiping his mouth on his sleeve, he put in another long day of prospecting.

"Hullo, Gus. Whenever you find that lucky vein of ore, I'm ready to pitch in," May reminded him. "I've been saving my pie and butter money to throw behind whoever finds the most promising claims, you know. I didn't come to this country to bake bread all my life."

"I'm a-trying, but these hills, they sure do hide their riches. I think maybe I'll head east to Wallace next."

"They say someone found a good outcropping of galena up there just two days ago."

"I heard that, too. Not sure it's true, though."

"It's worth a look, don't you think?"

"Yep, I do. Say, are you ready to head back? I'll carry your bucket for you. I promise I won't eat too many of your berries." Gus's eyes danced. "Or spill them. One stumble and they'd land on the rooftops down there."

"Thanks, Gus." May handed him her pail with a smile. It wasn't easy getting down these steep slopes with only one hand. Time after time, her scuffed old boots would slip and she'd fall on her backside. Still, the lure of these heavenly berries made her forget how tough the trip was. She could just smell the flaky brown crust and bubbling purple filling of tomorrow's pies and tarts. It was worth the climb.

"I sure am glad you came to this here valley, Miss Arkwright. I probably would've starved by now if I had to depend on my own cooking."

"Well, I love feeding you all, Gus. Cooking's what I do best, I guess. And I like those miners. They're a jolly lot. So many of them are just boys, really."

"Yep. They're all sure they're going to be rich."

"I feel right sorry for them, Gus. When they work in one of those company mines, they get worked to the bone." May grabbed a tree trunk to steady herself and continued her cautious trek down the mountainside. "I've been talking to them about labor unions and such. Nobody thinks about what would happen to them if they got hurt underground someplace. A union would take care of that. And what about better wages? Some of them have families to support."

"I dunno, Miss Arkwright. Folks around here hate them unions."

"I know they do, but damn it, Gus, unions are the only way everyday folks will get what they need."

"It seems to me those guys are too simple and scatterbrained to organize. But you're right. They sure get taken advantage of."

"Maybe someday, they'll see what I mean." May paused for a moment. They had almost reached the bottom of the slope. "Say, come by the diner tomorrow for a piece of huckleberry pie or a couple of tarts—your payment for carrying the bucket. I'd have spilled it for sure by now."

"That I'll gladly do."

May took the pail from Gus's work-roughened hands, said goodbye, and headed toward the diner. After she made the pies, she'd fetch the leather pouch hidden under the floorboard by her bed and count her coins. They added up after a while. Sooner or later, Gus Paulsen might find his wealth. He had perseverance. You never knew which of these rock outcroppings would turn out to be the mother lode. When it was discovered, she wanted to be ready. Then there would be no more scrubbing stew pots for a living.

CHAPTER 5

Al Hutton – Summer 1887

There was no doubt about it: May Arkwright was an intriguing woman.

He'd never known anyone quite like her. If he didn't watch himself, he could take a fancy to her—thunderous voice, hefty size, showy dresses, and all. The way he looked at it, she was confident and forthright, and above all, honest. He thought he'd caught a glimpse or two of vulnerability, too—something in her eyes when she talked about her upbringing— but maybe it was his imagination.

Oh, a lot of the folks out here were threatened by her overbearing ways. But if a man was certain of his own strength, a little power on the part of a woman didn't bother him. An independent woman was refreshing, especially when she was so warmhearted. She was smart, too; that was obvious. Early in the mornings when he went to her diner, he'd find her reading about politics or women's rights or workers' issues. Other days, she'd be memorizing poetry.

"Listen to this, Al," she'd say, and then, hands tucked into her colorful apron pockets, she'd recite a verse or two for him.

The men on the train teased him about his frequent visits to May's diner. "Heck, Al," they'd say. "With your looks, you could have any woman in the territory. That big homely Arkwright woman, she ain't your type." But what did they know about it?

He liked the way she favored the underdog—just like he did. Yesterday while he was eating her melt-in-your-mouth huckleberry flapjacks, she'd told him that she was really burned up that company mine owners didn't pay their miners a decent wage. Her cheeks flushed and her arms waved as she ranted about the dangerous conditions underground and how the workers were exploited.

Rumor had it she'd been married before, but he could understand that. It was lonely fending for yourself. He knew all about it. Maybe she'd married the first fellow who'd offered her a home, and it hadn't worked out. He'd ask her about it sometime.

She was tenderhearted, too. He'd never forget the day he stopped by the diner and found May kneeling on the floor bandaging a little boy's skinned knee. The tyke's haggard mother relaxed nearby, grasping a mug of coffee as if it were a lifeline. She was the one who had lost her husband in a mine cave-in the week before. The boy's face was streaked with tears, but his eyes were fixed on May's face as she gently washed and dressed his knee, all the while distracting him with an imaginative story about two squirrels, Bushy and Timmy—one bold and one timid—that lived in the woods nearby. Pretty soon, she had him laughing, and then she filled his pockets with enough cookies for a week.

As for May's looks, they didn't matter so much. She carried all that weight with a certain buoyant gracefulness. Her clothes amused him, but he had to admire her pluck in wearing them. Those rumpled low-collared gowns were a little comical. Some of them didn't adequately cover her creamy neck. He tried not to glance there when they were talking; common decency demanded that. Those sights were for married men, not a lonely train engineer who took a liking to his breakfast cook. But he enjoyed the bright reds, yellows, and blues she wore, the ruffles and ribbons and lace, and those outlandish hats. Other women, in their properly muted colors and modest necklines, looked pale and uninteresting.

May didn't mince her words, and he respected her for it. She was as plainspoken and straightforward as a child, so he knew he could trust her. While other women practiced coy glances and white-gloved gestures, May filled up a room with her loud voice and uncensored language. She said exactly what she thought, and if something amused her, she didn't titter behind her hand, but instead let loose with a big, hearty guffaw. While the upscale Wardner ladies spent time curling their bangs and keeping their parlors clean, May was pushing for woman suffrage and labor unions.

She was filled with life, May was. She had flair and compassion. A man could overlook her faults.

CHAPTER 6

Summer 1887

OH, HECK. THESE BEANS HAD SOAKED ALL NIGHT, BUT SHE HAD FORGOT-
ten she was out of salt pork. Even with plenty of onion and molasses, the
baked beans wouldn't taste right without it. There was enough time before
dinner for a trip to the grocer's if she dashed.

She grabbed her hat and hurried up the street, intent on her errand.
Honky-tonk music and acrid cigar smoke spilled from the saloons. May
nodded to a couple of tipsy pedestrians. Two freckle-faced boys played
marbles in the mud, oblivious to the horse droppings nearby. She turned a
corner and caught sight of one of the townswomen dressed in an expensive beige gown, heading toward her, carefully watching where she was
placing her feet as she crossed the mucky street. How nice to see a woman's face in this town full of men!

They reached the grocer's door at the same moment. May smiled.
"Howdy! Good to see you out today!"

The woman froze and raised her eyes from the muddy ground to
May's face. Her sweeping glance took in May's scuffed shoes and ample
work dress. Recognition registered on her face as she met May's eyes
briefly. Then she stepped back as if affronted. Her gloved hand fluttered
to her throat as she turned and hurried away without speaking.

May swallowed. A red flush spread over her face and neck. That was a fine how-do-you-do! What had she done to deserve a snub like that?

"And a nice day to you, too!" she hollered, her voice shaking with anger. Just wait until she made her fortune! She'd show these high and mighty folks who thought they were too good to pass the time of day with May Arkwright!

She stood in the doorway, trembling for a few minutes, before she gave herself a little shake. Those snobs didn't deserve her time anyhow. She sure as hell didn't want to be friends with people who judged others by their clothes, their manners, or who their parents were.

It hurt, though. She felt the sting in that soft spot deep inside that she rarely let anyone see.

May squared her shoulders and stepped into the store. She had better things to do than fret. The miners would be showing up for their baked beans soon. She'd better take care of her shopping and head back to the diner.

Hurrying home with the salt pork in her bag, she noticed black clouds moving in from the west. "Thunder boomers" they were called here, and that was no lie. She'd learned a thing or two about storms here in Idaho Territory. Jim Wardner had been right: They hit with such force that the walls shook. The sharp cracks of thunder made her jump out of her skin. In between, the rumble was deafening, echoing off the mountainsides the way it did.

Here she was a grown woman, and she dreaded thunderstorms like a child.

Back home, Granddad used to let her sit at the foot of his rocking chair as lightning flashed and thunder roared around his house. His gnarled hand would stroke her head as he told stories to distract her. Those were some of her best childhood memories. She never told anyone, but sometimes, even now, when a storm hit in the night and she was alone in the darkness, she gently smoothed her own hair over and over, just as Granddad had done.

When her parents left, he had taken over her care—or rather, she had taken over his. Without his eyesight, he had a heck of a time cooking, cleaning, or gardening. Ten-year-old May had done that herself. And even though the old man did his best, he couldn't tell if May had scrubbed her face or if her dress was getting dingy. She figured out in a hurry how to sew her own simple skirts and bodices, which Granddad insisted must be properly plain and drab. Maybe that was why she loved to fancy up her clothes now.

People told her she was indomitable. She liked to think she was. Still, on a day like this, when it seemed the world rejected her, she missed Granddad until her heart ached. Her chest tightened, just thinking about it.

In the distance, Al Hutton's distinctive train whistle blew. May looked around, but he was too far off to see. Still, as she strode back to the diner her mood lifted. There were plenty of good-hearted, decent people here she could count on.

CHAPTER 7

Late Summer 1887

OH, IT FELT GOOD TO HOLD A MAN'S ARM AGAIN. MAY TUCKED HER HAND under Al's elbow as they made their way along the dirty railroad track. Ever since Bert had left her—and then went and got himself drowned— she'd hoped for a companionable man to take his place.

She took a deep breath. It was one thing for Al to show up at her eatery day after day along with the usual crowd of miners. It was quite another for him to ask her to go walking. Outdoors on this balmy summer day, the whole world could see them strolling arm in arm. That meant only one thing in her book.

She sneaked a sidelong glance at his face. Chiseled. Wasn't that the word those dime novels used to describe the handsome hero? It fit Al perfectly. His face was a series of fine, even planes. She liked the way his light-brown hair curled over the collar of his gray work shirt, too, and how his eyes, tucked under those bushy eyebrows, sometimes twinkled with kindness or humor.

Heck, she could keep herself guessing all day about why a man like Al would want to take her out walking. Certainly it couldn't be her appearance, although she'd worn her favorite dress for the occasion. And it couldn't be her social graces; every other woman in Wardner Junction ran circles around her in that area. She'd never been one for convention and silly formalities. Maybe Al liked her way of making easy conversation—or maybe just her home cooking.

"So why do people call you Al if your real name is Levi?" May squinted in the sunlight, watching where she placed her feet. Al was steering her up the hill toward the main street.

"Same reason they call you May when your real name is Mary." Al smiled at her. "For short, I guess. It got started after my folks died."

"You were an orphan!"

"Yep. My uncle raised me—or he tried. I left when I was barely old enough to make a sparse living on my own."

"I was an orphan, too." No wonder they were drawn to each other! "Well, sort of. I had my nice old granddad to raise me. My ma and pa, though, they left when I was ten. I don't know if I'd recognize my ma if she came walking down the street toward us." May's voice wavered almost imperceptibly, and she stopped. "Hold up for a minute, Al. I've got to catch my breath."

"I knew your grandpa raised you. You told me one morning at the diner. But you said you took care of him, too. He was blind or something."

"He couldn't see that piercing headlight on your locomotive. Things were as black as the inside of a coal bin for him. Back in Ohio, I used to walk him downtown so he could visit his friends. And he liked political rallies. Sometimes he'd invite the speaker home with us—I would make them my homemade doughnuts—and I'd spend the evening listening to the two of them talk about political issues."

"That's why you get so fussed up by the way things are for the miners here."

"You're darned right. It's a sickening shame how they're treated. I came here to get rich, like most folks. I do want to be well-off, but not just for myself. I want to be able to help all those poor souls out there in the world."

"Like orphans?"

"Orphans. Miners. Lots of others. I've already bought interests in a couple of mines, and I'm saving now so I can invest again."

He looked down at her. "You're a smart woman, May. Buying interests might pay off someday. I've invested some of my wages the same way. Maybe we'll get lucky."

"I sure as heck hope so. Mighty few do, though."

"Most people aren't as determined as you."

They started moving again, and Al guided her right up the main street of Wardner Junction. May hoped every last one of the snooty ladies who lived there was looking through her lace-curtained window. She, May Arkwright, was strolling up the street on the arm of the handsomest, most eligible man in the territory.

"There are a few things you need to know about me, Al," she said, hurrying on before he could respond. "I had to quit school after only a few terms. I've been married before. And I won't kowtow to any man." There. She'd said it. Now if Al Hutton wanted to take her places, he'd know the full story. There'd be no surprises. He could turn and run if he wanted.

"Well, I'm no advanced student myself, and I like a woman with a little spunk. The rest is water under the bridge, as far as I'm concerned."

Water under the bridge. What a kind way to put it. And spunk? Is that what he liked? She could show him spunk. That was something she had in great supply. The sun felt warmer on her face, and birds chirped from the treetops as they reached the end of the street. She turned and looked at him. This time he returned her gaze. His eyes weren't twinkling now; they were as calm and serious as she'd ever seen them.

"That's nice of you, Al," she said simply.

He shrugged. "Life's too uncertain to let things get in the way."

She nodded. Suddenly her knees were weak and she was ravenous.

"Come on, let's turn around. I've got a good, old-fashioned stew on the back of the stove, and there's pie, too." That was something else she had in great supply—endless skill at turning out pies and delicious dishes. She could take an old piece of venison or a plain mound of flour and transform it into a tender, savory roast or a tray of heavenly tarts. "No berries this time of year, but I had some apples and cinnamon and sugar. I'll warm a big slice for you."

It was late when Al finally left the diner. Undressing for bed in the darkness, May wondered where the time had gone. Tonight they had talked until they outlasted the oil in the lamp, which burned out with a puff of smoke and left them in blackness. Al gave her hand a squeeze before he fumbled his way to the door.

"That's our cue, I guess," he remarked, and May could hear the grin in his voice. "Time flies when you're having fun. Good night, May."

She was too keyed up to fall asleep. She thought back over their conversation, marveling at all the things she and Al agreed on. It seemed as though they could talk about anything, and tonight they had: memories from childhood, what it was like to drive a train, why each had come to Idaho Territory, ways to weatherproof the diner, why she loved poetry so much. She'd learned a lot about Al's orphan days and his early railroading in Missoula.

She couldn't remember when she had enjoyed a day more. It made a woman think.

CHAPTER 8

Autumn 1887

ALL THROUGH THE GOLDEN FALL, MAY HAD AL'S MIDDAY DINNER READY when the locomotive screeched to a halt outside the diner. Al would swing to the ground while the engine idled and give her a quick hug as she handed him a wrapped plate of hearty beefsteak and buttery mashed potatoes, or a mess of those tasty trout from the river. Once, when the supply wagon brought a watermelon from Spokane, she doled out sweet slices to no one but Al. In her spare moments, she took to sewing handkerchiefs for him from leftover scraps of white petticoat fabric. She bound the edges with her expert whip stitches and then embroidered his name in black in the center.

Al brought May little gifts in return: a yard of cream-colored lace from the dry goods store, a perfect squash from a passenger's garden, and a shiny lump of silvery-gray galena. As he offered them to her, he would clasp her hand for a moment and look into her eyes. He never said much, but May figured she knew a man's feelings when she saw them.

She felt like a schoolgirl these days. Not that she got silly and sentimental, but Al was such an uncommon man. She'd never known anyone who felt her passion for helping folks like he did, and who wasn't mortified by her outbursts of temper. When God created Al Hutton, He added an extra dose of kindness and understanding. Maybe that made Al a bit

28

of an outcast, too, here in Wardner Junction, where men often used their fists more than their brains. He was tough—there was no doubt about that—but he was more than that. Along with his engineer's muscles, he had a head on his shoulders and a tender heart beating in his chest.

May shoved up her sleeves to begin kneading dough. It was cold as the devil in here this afternoon, even with the stove burning hot. She was glad she had put up that gingham curtain. It trapped the heat and gave her the only shred of privacy she had. Miners lounged at the front table all evening after gulping down their suppers, laughing and telling stories until she kicked them out. Most times she sat with them after she served the pie, but once in a while she just collapsed on her plank bed in the back and blocked out the sounds of their shouted laughter. It was a darned good thing she loved to cook, because feeding all those men was enough to wear anyone out.

If she could just get this dough finished, she'd have time for a quick trip to the privy. The thought made her shiver. By gosh, someday she'd have an indoor privy and not have to sit on that icy seat. She pushed aside the curly strand of brown hair that hung across her forehead and wiped her hands on her floury apron. An indoor privy wouldn't be pitch-black inside, either, and there would be no slippery path to stumble down at night.

She divided the dough and set the pans to rise near the stove, avoiding the knotholes in the wall where the chill blew in. There was an art to making decent bread, and she'd perfected it even in this rough place.

She had her back to the door when she heard it open, and a blast of cold air gusted in.

"Come in and shut the damned door!" May bellowed, and then turned to look, expecting the first of the dirt-covered miners. Instead, two strangers stood there, hats in hands, staring at her dumbfounded. May gave a chuckle. "Excuse my language, gentlemen. But that's an icy wind you were letting in."

"Uh . . . could we get a bite of supper here?" The taller of the two men finally spoke up. His dark wool pants were covered with dust, but he wore a formal buttoned vest under his coat.

"I've got hot potato soup with plenty of bread and butter. Take it or leave it."

"Sounds good to me," the man said, stepping to the table. "I'm Harry Day and this here's Fred Harper."

"I'm May Arkwright. Nice to meet you, gentlemen. Are you new to these parts?"

"No, just doing some prospecting. We've taken a good look at the mines here, mostly the Wardelena, because we aim to find the next one."

"Well, I hope you do. If you happen upon it, let me know. Have you been looking up Chinook Gulch?"

"Nope, we've spent our days up in the . . ." Fred shot Harry a warning glance. ". . . well, you know, just up in the hills."

"I know very well you don't care to let on where you've been. That's smart. No telling how many prospectors are out there and they all want to be the first to discover something."

"You heard any rumors? Any talk?" Fred asked. "You must get a lot of people passing through here."

"Well, you can ask them yourselves. There's a good crowd of men that takes supper here. They'll be busting through the door any minute, coated with dirt and full of loud talk. Most of them work at the Bunker Hill and Sullivan mines. You'll have to move over to make room. I've got more benches outside if we need 'em."

As she spoke, the door opened again and Gus Paulsen stepped in. He glanced at the strangers, nodded, and sat on an upended log at the table.

"Hullo, Gus." May set a cup of coffee in front of him. "This is Harry Day and Fred Harper. They're prospecting for a new mine."

Gus's head shot up, but he greeted them and said nothing more. Pretty soon he got up and went outside to fetch the extra benches.

Harry Day. Fred Harper. She'd do well to memorize those names. It wouldn't hurt to know every prospector in the valley, now, would it? She ladled the steaming soup into bowls and cut thick slices of bread. The rest of the loaf she wrapped in a clean piece of brown paper. Maybe with an extra portion of her crusty bread in their saddlebags, they'd remember May Arkwright and come back here to eat. Maybe they'd be the ones to make her a fortune in the mines.

CHAPTER 9

Al Hutton – Autumn 1887

May had told him she didn't feel accepted here, but the truth was she had a hundred friends. They weren't the upper-crust ladies from town, but May had a following like no other: downhearted miners, the old woman up the gulch who raised chickens, scruffy-looking prospectors, a couple of painted ladies. There were others, too: leaders like Jim Wardner, and that politician from Spokane, and even that Republican lawmaker back East she'd met—the one who was thinking of running for president. May made friends wherever she went.

When the two of them went for their Sunday walks, men hollered their hellos to her from the saloons, and children ran to hold her hand. More than once, May had asked him to deliver a fried chicken or a hand-knitted scarf to a young widow she knew. On picnics, they almost always bumped into some-one who joined them for a slice of pie. Most times, people came to her diner to talk. He had learned—after a couple of quick jabs of jealousy—that if he walked into the diner to find May leaning across the table intent on another man's face, she was listening, not flirting. The most discreet thing to do was to retreat to the benches outside. After a while, sometimes quite a while, he would hear May's skillet clatter on the stovetop and would go in for breakfast.

When she entered a room, most folks would smile at her and then lean back in their chairs and call out a joke or two. Maybe her big voice, plain face, and down-to-earth manners made people feel she was one of them. Maybe it was because she paid attention and really heard their stories, looking deep into their eyes as they talked. Sometimes she'd even take a person's hand in her own. It breached every rule of etiquette, but folks loved that warm touch.

Of course he'd noticed the demure wives of mine owners and bankers act as if they didn't see her when she barreled down the street. Once he watched a silk-clad lady hurry her children into a store to avoid saying hello. In his book, that didn't mean a thing. Far more important was the way May sought out folks who were having troubles—and then lifted them up with her genuine goodwill. She had a heart of gold, May did.

She'd had a tough life so far. It was one thing to become an orphan because your parents died, like his own. It was quite another to be abandoned. Thinking about it made his throat close. May was too busy to dwell on her childhood, but a couple of times he thought he detected mist in her eyes when they talked about it. Thank goodness for that old granddad of hers. He'd given her a home and plenty of solid influence.

It didn't take much to make May happy. She looked at this ugly settlement of Wardner Junction and saw only the potential. The rough life out here—the pack rats, the icy winters, the long days of drudgery—didn't faze her a bit. And she was as thrilled as a girl with the silly little presents he gave her. A few Sundays ago when they were out walking, he'd picked a handful of wild daisies, braided them into a crown, and nestled it onto her head. She'd worn it all day, even while serving dinner. When the miners ribbed her about it, she just smiled and, for once, didn't say a word. He realized right then that he could make her happy—not only in little ways, but in big ones, too.

He'd courted her for weeks, but he'd known from the start. May Arkwright was the woman for him. Enough of the picnics and town dances and Sunday strolls. It was far too soon for convention's sake, but he'd better get moving and ask her to marry him, or someone else would.

CHAPTER 10

Autumn 1887

MAY PULLED HER ROYAL-BLUE DRESS OVER HER HEAD AND PUT HER ARMS in the sleeves. That piece of lace Al brought her last week sure did look nice stitched onto her cuffs. She liked to imagine him in the dry goods store picking it out for her. Heck, what other man would do that? She'd wear this dress today, even if it was a little fancy for an autumn picnic, just to show him she appreciated it. She'd start out with a hat, too, maybe the one with the white silk roses. Later, she'd take it off to feel the sun on her face and the breeze in her hair. An extra hairpin or two would hold her long brown hair low on her neck, although Al didn't mind if she just let it flutter loose. She loved to feel the cool wind lifting her curls with a gentle tugging. Sometimes, if he knew they were alone, Al would reach over and secure a wayward strand behind her ear.

He sure was proper in his displays of affection. Oh, he held her hand often enough and sometimes even put his arm around her waist. She knew his good manners were customary, but sometimes she wished he'd hurry up and be a little more familiar. Maybe she'd have to lead the way. Having been married back in Ohio, she probably knew more about such things anyhow. So far Al had only kissed her twice, and one of those kisses had been on her cheek. Even that had left her breathless and giddy.

She glanced out the window. There he was now, making his way toward the diner to pick her up. He looked more dressed up than usual in a high-collared white shirt and his black coat and trousers. Her heart beat faster. Honestly, she never failed to be amazed that a man so good looking was interested in her. He knew his mind, though, even if she couldn't fathom it. So she just kept on being herself and he kept on coming around.

"Ready to go?" Al took the picnic basket from her. "This smells good."

"It's your favorite. I fried up a chicken."

"Oh, you do spoil me, May." He smiled and then touched her sleeve, noticing the lace.

They ambled down to the river. Old cottonwoods lined its banks, stretching golden branches over the water and releasing their balsamlike fragrance into the air. Underfoot, the ground was dry, but a few late-summer wildflowers lingered in the shade. A squirrel chattered at them as they passed and a magpie let out its raucous call. Al found an old game trail that meandered along the water's edge, and they followed it downstream. He led the way, stopping now and then to hold a low branch aside for her, until they came to a shaded clearing. A sudden breeze sent a shower of yellow leaves floating to the ground. One of the giant old trees had fallen, leaving its trunk to act as a bench. May spread her shawl over the gnarled bark and scooted herself onto it, saving the more comfortable spot for Al. She took off her hat and set it beside her.

Boy, oh boy, it was peaceful out here. From where they sat they could see the mountains on the far side of the valley. She could stay here forever with this man, watching the river glide by.

Al cleared his throat and thrust his hand into his pocket, then withdrew it and sat beside her. "Shall we break out the picnic?"

"Sure. I forgot napkins, though. This chicken's going to be a little messy."

"We'll share my handkerchief."

"I'd like to share a lot more with you than just your hankie, Al Hutton."

He grinned. "Good, May Arkwright. I'd like that, too." He bit into a drumstick and sat chewing for a moment. Then he swallowed and wiped his fingers. "I need to tell you something."

Her heart skipped a beat.

"They're putting in railroad tracks to that latest ore discovery up Canyon Creek north of Wallace," he said. "The new mines up there near Burke need a train. It's a grim little canyon, though, narrow and steep, and it gets a terrible amount of snow in winter. The Northern Pacific needs an experienced engineer to manage the grade. That's me. They told me they're going to give me the route."

May stopped chewing. Wallace was twelve miles away.

"I'll be stationed at Wallace," Al went on, looking out over the river. "That means I might not be coming to Wardner Junction much."

The fried chicken stuck in her throat. She swallowed, but there was still a big lump there. Twelve miles! It might as well be a thousand. Her eyes filled. She reached out to grab Al's hankie from his hand, but he grasped her fingers and held on.

"So I've been thinking." Al set his plate down and stood up. Then he kneeled in the dirt in front of her. "May, I . . . I'd like to ask you to marry me."

Oh, good Lord in Heaven! She tried to take a breath. Al—solid, kind, handsome, wonderful Al Hutton—was proposing to her!

"You don't have to answer me now. It would mean you'd have to give up the diner and move to Wallace. I know that wouldn't be easy." Al reached up and wiped a tear from her cheek. May closed her eyes, and suddenly Al was standing, pulling her to her feet. His arms went around her, drawing her close, and he kissed her slowly. Then he said softly, "I'd be a happy man if you said yes."

May slipped her arms around his neck. This must be what heaven felt like—to be enfolded in Al's arms and feel his tender kiss in her very core. She could hear his quick breathing and feel his muscled shoulders and broad back. Her knees trembled. She would love Al forever, she knew it. She reached up and stroked his rough face while she found her voice.

"Yes! Oh, good Lord, yes! I'll marry you, Al." Then she softened her tone. "I'd be honored."

He smiled. "And I'd be honored to have you as my wife." He reached into his pocket. "I've got something for you. It's the prettiest one I could find in Spokane." He opened a small, satin-lined box and slipped a ring onto her finger.

Oh, Al knew her, all right. It was just what she might have chosen for herself, a filigreed silver setting surrounding a sparkling blue sapphire. But at that moment, the ring didn't matter at all. What mattered was that Al Hutton, with his gentle manners and good sense and strong, dependable ways, had asked her to marry him.

"Oh, Al. Thank you." She looked into his eyes—those steadfast gray eyes that met hers without wavering. "I love you."

"And I love you, May. Now and forever."

CHAPTER 11

Early November 1887

MAY SAT AT THE TABLE WITH WEDDING INVITATIONS SPREAD OUT ON the red oilcloth. Thin afternoon sunlight slanted through the window. She fingered the ivory-colored paper with pleasure as she wrote names on the envelopes. What a celebration this would be!

Scooting closer to the glowing stove, she put down her fountain pen and made a mental list of things that needed to be done, and fast. Al's courtship had been brief—better measured in weeks than months—but they had decided to get married right away. No sense wasting time, especially when Al had to start work in Wallace soon. The wedding would be this month—November 17, to be exact—right here in Wardner Junction.

This time, she thought, she would have a proper affair with a real ordained minister, a fancy new dress, and mountains of food for the guests.

She could make her own dress, or . . . did she dare order one from Spokane? The cost might bowl her over, but one thing was certain: She wanted the latest fashion, with a bustle. Of course, she didn't need any big bustle accentuating her backside. But how could she let Al marry someone with no sense of style? A soft pastel color would be nice, too—maybe a pale pink or blue.

Land sakes, imagine marrying Al Hutton! She hadn't felt like this when she and Bert had gotten hitched back home. With Al, she had no doubt whatsoever. Why, the two of them could talk for hours and it seemed like a few fleeting moments. They went about their lives in a completely different fashion, but they always agreed on the things that mattered. And underneath all that compatibility there was a physical pull between the two of them. She knew Al felt it too. When they were together, it hung in the air like the charged feeling just before a thunderstorm.

A loud bawling interrupted her thoughts. It was old Emma, grazing behind the diner. She needed milking again. With a sigh, May got to her feet, pulled on her shawl, and grabbed the tin bucket. She'd wanted her own cow so she'd have fresh cream and butter for the diner. But the labor of it all! Twice a day without fail she had to milk, no matter if it was pouring rain or blowing a blizzard. She loved Emma, whom she'd named after the Jane Austen book she'd just finished, but sometimes May felt like giving her to anyone who'd take her.

May leaned her head against the cow's warm flank and squirted milk into the pail. Al was getting the parson for the wedding. For all of his rough upbringing, her husband-to-be sure was proper. Maybe it was the Masons that made him value respectability. He'd been a Mason ever since he started railroading in Missoula, and it seemed to May that the organization was his anchor. He liked their cigar-smoking companionship and emphasis on civic duty.

She nudged Emma aside, took the sloshing pail, and went back indoors. The miners would be tromping in for supper soon. She didn't have time to finish the invitations, so she scooped them up and put them in the back room. They were sure to raise some eyebrows. She'd dropped the Munn name when she came to Idaho, hoping for a fresh start. Nonetheless, the invitations read "the wedding of Mrs. May Arkwright Munn to Mr. Levi W. Hutton." She wasn't sure why she had used the "Mrs." and her old married name, but it had something to do with showing the world exactly who she was. That, and the miners who had traveled out west with her knew her history anyhow. Folks could think what they wanted.

She had already mailed one back home to Ohio. Her distant half-siblings would be surprised that she was marrying again, especially Lyman, the oldest, with whom she kept in occasional touch. They'd been shocked at her decision to go West without a chaperone, and remarriage probably wasn't in their code of proper behavior either. But, hell, they needed to know.

Al had already asked his friend E. D. Osier to stand up for him. She debated who to choose for her maid of honor. She knew plenty of womenfolk here, but the one person she wanted to ask was too far away—clear up over the mountains in Murrayville. Having Molly Burdan (or Molly B'Dam, as the miners affectionately called her) in the wedding would raise a lot of eyebrows because of her red-light profession, but in May's mind, Molly was the kindest, most generous woman in Idaho Territory. They had met back in Eagle City when they both first arrived. Never a day went by when Molly didn't do a good deed for someone. When all those folks got sick over there in Murrayville, Molly nursed them tirelessly. May could just see her slipping quietly from cabin to cabin in her wool shawl and big hat, her pretty face pulled into a frown of concern, carrying whatever would bring comfort for smallpox. Molly would help anyone, anywhere. Too bad she was twenty impossible miles away.

Maybe Grace Hoskins would do instead. Grace was a pert, friendly woman and the closest thing May had to a female kindred spirit here in Wardner Junction. Women mostly didn't come to the diner alone, and May toiled over her stove nearly eighteen hours a day, but the two of them had shared many a conversation in the dry goods store and on group picnics. She'd go find Grace and ask her tomorrow.

If she had anything to say about it, every wedding guest would go home satisfied from a real feast. She would begin baking her pies—apple, pumpkin, vinegar, and even sour cream raisin if she could get the raisins—a day ahead. They would stay chilled in the unheated lean-to that abutted the diner. The hard part would be the oyster stew and wild duck with all the trimmings, she guessed. Those would have to be made on her wedding day.

There would be no liquor, though. That was another thing she and Al agreed on. Neither one of them drank; they'd seen what a few shots of whiskey could do to others. No, there would be coffee and tea and maybe a nice chokecherry punch, but no spirits at all.

Al had helped her with a big bouquet for the table. One sunny October day they had wandered the hillsides and riverbank, snapping off the most eye-catching dried leaves and flowers they could find. She had them hanging from the ceiling now—a big, showy spray of pale straw flowers, golden grass tassels, the picture-perfect teasel that grew in the marshland, and yellow aspen and cottonwood leaves she had pressed with her flatiron to preserve their color. Bunched together, they made a dazzling arrangement, if she did say so herself. Maybe she'd choose a few to make herself a bouquet to carry.

Reluctantly, she began slicing onions to fry for the supper crowd. By the time the first miners were seated, her eyes were running, making it look as though she were crying. But her heart was soaring, and she hummed a little song as she tossed the slices into the sizzling pan.

CHAPTER 12

Thanksgiving Day, November 17, 1887

THE WEDDING DAY WAS COLD AND CLEAR. MAY COULD TELL HER FACE was flushed as she poked more firewood into the diner's stove. A puff of smoke made her cough and slam the black iron door with a clang. She rubbed her stinging eyes and turned to survey the front room. Last night, Al had helped her move the table to the wall and sweep the splintery plank floor. They'd hauled in the outdoor benches and arranged them, with the chairs and upended stumps, along the walls. There was room for quite a little crowd in here now.

May grabbed her old stained apron from its hook and tied it around her middle. What to do first? There was plenty of time before people started arriving; she'd made sure of that. She hated scurrying around at the last minute getting flustered because she wasn't ready. Unfurling the new tablecloth she'd made—yellow cotton from the end of a bolt—she spread it over the everyday oilcloth. It brightened the room considerably. The table was sturdy enough that the entire wedding feast could be spread out there.

She brought the pies from the lean-to and put them near the stove to warm. Then she fetched the dried bouquet hanging overhead and took it outside, where it wouldn't mess up her clean floor while she arranged it in a big empty jar, adding the dark-brown cattails Al brought by yesterday.

Heck, this was as good as any fancy flowers. She picked up the whole shebang carefully, took it inside, set it on the table, and stood back to admire her work.

May kept one eye on the angle of the sun as she slid the plucked wild turkey and plump duck into the oven, milked Emma, set aside the creamy milk for oyster stew, and quickly kneaded dough for the rolls. The preserves and pickles were ready to set out. Butter was staying cool in the lean-to. She'd made fresh applesauce yesterday, and Grace was bringing the beans. The yellow squash could go in the oven later, as long as she didn't forget in the last-minute hustle. And the glazed wedding cake, rich with nuts and fruit, was ready and waiting.

Her colorful patchwork quilt was smoothed carefully over the mattress. She'd washed and dried it yesterday, because Al would be staying over tonight, of course. Next, she would bathe. She wanted to be clean from head to toe, because she intended to show Al Hutton a thing or two about being married.

Baths were always a little tricky. May filled her round washtub with a bucketful of cold creek water and then hot water from the kettle, and started by leaning over the side to lather her hair. After scooping water into an old jar and pouring it over her head to rinse away the soap, she tousled her dripping hair with flour sacking. Shivering, she undressed and squeezed herself into the tub to wash the rest of her. It was a chore, indeed. A once-a-week ordeal.

When she was finally done, she put on her underclothes and pulled a chair close to the stove to brush out her hair and let it dry in the heat. Al would be here in an hour, and after him, Grace and Ed, their attendants. Then the guests would begin to come. She wasn't sure of the exact number, but she and Al had invited quite a few. It would be a tight squeeze fitting them all in the diner, but they'd manage. Thank goodness it wasn't pouring rain; afterward some of the men could step outside to smoke and talk, even if it was wintery and cold.

Her hands were clammy as she pulled on her petticoat and then fumbled with the row of pearly buttons that cascaded down the front of her plush pale-blue wedding dress—a Spokane gown cut princess-style in the latest fashion and sporting an elaborate bustle, just as she had wanted. She could tell it looked nice, accentuating her curves as it did. She brushed her hair until it gleamed and piled it in a loose chignon, adding a white velvet hat embellished with lace. As she adjusted the hairpins, there was a knock on the door.

Al stood there in his best black trousers and jacket. The starched collar of the white shirt he'd ordered was set off by a black tie. His hair was parted straight down the center and slicked back, and his usually straight mouth was turned up in a grin. May opened her mouth to speak, but no words came out. Al took one look at her, stepped back, and then let his gaze travel all the way from her shoes to her face. He reached out to touch the velvety softness of her sleeve.

"You look stunning," he said finally, looking into her eyes. "Stunning. I'm a happy man today." He came forward and took her in his arms. She stayed there, quiet, leaning her head on his shoulder with her face turned toward his so her hat wouldn't scratch his cheek. She nestled her hands on his warm chest and closed her eyes. A lump tried to force its way into her throat, but she swallowed it away.

"I'm happy, too, dear. More happy than I can ever remember."

"Well, well. Look at the lovebirds!" E. D. Osier rounded the corner of the building with Grace Hoskins on his arm. "Mind if we interrupt? We've brought you a gift and a proposition."

Al stepped away, and May blurted out, "I didn't know you two were . . . friends!"

"We're more than just friends. In fact, that's our proposition," Ed laughed, handing Al a parcel tied with string. "We'd like to share your wedding—I mean, get married ourselves. Would you mind?" He winked at Al and added, "We could share the wedding gifts, too, right, old buddy?"

Al looked at May as if to read her thoughts. "Not the gifts, old man. The wedding, maybe."

May took a breath. Now here was a strange turn of events. She didn't even realize Grace and Ed knew each other, and here they were ready to tie the knot. But, heck, why not? Everything was set for one wedding. Adding another set of vows wouldn't change much. She smiled. "Grace, you scoundrel! I had no idea!"

"Ed just now asked! And how can a girl say no?" Grace giggled as she glanced up at her beau. "I sure didn't think I'd be getting married today, but if you don't mind, May . . ."

"I guess so. All right with you, Al?"

"Yep. It's fine with me. You folks go first, though. I want to save the best for last." He looked lingeringly at May again.

Glancing down the road, May could see the preacher's horse plodding closer and couples strolling along the railroad tracks toward the diner. Far in the distance, Gus Paulsen's milk wagon lumbered along the road, its roomy platform filled with people.

Before long, the little diner was bursting with guests, and May had to shut down the stove to keep it from getting stuffy. She and Al stood at the door, welcoming the crowd. "Howdy, Jim! Come on in, there's room for everyone. Hullo, Fred! Miss Daisy, welcome." Voices grew louder as the room filled.

Then, before she knew it, she was standing by the window with Al, holding tight to his lean hand to steady herself. For some reason, she was trembling all over. Al could tell, and his eyes twinkled as he gently squeezed her chapped fingers. In front of them, the bearded preacher held his worn black Bible and peered at the pages through spectacles balanced on his nose. Behind them, the guests were crowded into a knot: a motley mixture of disheveled miners, trainmen, customers from the diner, and community leaders. There were a few young women wearing too much rouge, and two merchants with their mousy wives, but no relatives had made the journey. May didn't mind that there were no kinfolk. Al was all she needed. She smiled at him and he smiled back as the minister began to speak.

There, smack-dab in the Silver Valley of Idaho Territory, they were married. May repeated her vows with gusto. She looked straight into Al's eyes as she spoke, and for once in her life, she saw love looking back at her. Al was a gem. She would keep him forever, and she said so—loud and clear, so that everyone could hear.

CHAPTER 13

December 1887

MAY GAVE A CONTENTED SIGH AS SHE GLANCED OUT THE LOG CABIN'S window. Being married to Al was just as it should be. He treated her like a queen, making it clear that she was an equal partner, not some simpleton he expected to fix meals and pick up after him. They'd been married a month, and already she knew that teaming up with Al Hutton was the best thing she'd ever done.

She opened the door and stepped outside with her broom. The sloping porch was covered with three inches of powdery new snow, even beneath the overhanging roof. Small flakes whirled around her as an icy wind pressed her long black work dress against her legs. Shivering, she quickly swept the rough planks clean, her breath turning to white puffs of frost. The light was fading, and the woods around her had taken on the dark blue of evening. She took a deep breath. The frosty air pinched her nostrils but held the fragrance of evergreens and fresh snow. A crow, cawing raucously, flew through the trees.

From where she stood, she could look down on the whole town of Wallace. Although it was still a primitive mining camp hacked out of the wilderness, it was beginning to resemble a bustling little town. Snowy streets and boardwalks connected unpainted wooden buildings, which were lined up in an orderly grid, and wood smoke made plumes from every chimney. Men hurried among the buildings, avoiding the alleys that were still just piles of brush and stumps. Even on a cold day like this, May could hear the muffled blows of hammers and the occasional thud of a new board being dropped into place. And across the narrow valley was the slit in the mountains—Canyon Creek—that boasted the railroad to Burke. Somewhere up there out of sight, Al was probably shoveling coal into the locomotive's firebox in preparation for the trip back to Wallace. May shivered again before she turned and hurried back inside.

Putting the broom near the stove to dry, she warmed her hands over its hot surface and then turned around to thaw her backside. This cabin was darned cozy, considering that it was perched on the steepest, darkest mountainside she'd ever seen. She lighted the lamps and watched the flickering light brighten the roughhewn log walls. There was time to work on the curtains before Al got home. Even though the cabin had only two windows—one in each room—they felt stark and cold without some muslin ruffles to cover them. Taking her needle from the pincushion, she pulled her rocking chair closer to the stove and took up her stitching.

Al was sure gone a lot. Coaxing the locomotive up the gulch kept him busy for long hours. At first, May had been content to unpack their things and set up housekeeping. It had been fun to blend their belongings together, sort of like mixing cinnamon and sugar into a pretty, swirly concoction. She had arranged Al's prized reading lamp on the worn table from the diner that now sat in the front room. His battered lunch bucket went beside her big wicker basket. In the small bedroom, she hung his frayed work clothes beside her own lacy dresses and set her oak hairbrush and Al's black comb on the tiny nightstand.

Married life was still too new for her to be bored, exactly. So far, she hadn't made many trips downtown; it wasn't easy getting to the stores below and then panting your way back home again. But she was used to working day and night, cooking for the crowds of miners. Now there wasn't quite enough to do, especially since it was winter. It was true she had time to visit her neighbors, though they were few and far between, and to cook up special dinners for Al. And she finally had time to read. In fact, she was devouring every book she could get her hands on—history, politics, literature—that would help make up for her lack of proper schooling. Still, some days the hours dragged by, and she was afraid she overwhelmed Al with her need for companionship when he came home, tired and sooty, from the train.

"Give me just a minute to wash up, May, and then you can talk all you want," he'd say. But she knew that her quiet husband sometimes needed a little silence, so after dinner she'd pick up her book again and let him have his peace.

On Sundays, they spent more time together. May cooked up a big breakfast, and Al went about his weekly chores while she washed up. He'd knock the heavy icicles from the eaves, shovel the walkway to the privy, and chop firewood. Then he'd warm his hands by the stove for a few minutes before suggesting a walk to town. May was more than happy to oblige. The old-timers talked about cabin fever, and she was beginning to understand what they meant.

"Here's what I've been thinking," she told him one cold Sunday afternoon as they strolled through Wallace. "I'd like to get a job."

"Whatever you want is fine by me," he answered. "It's your happiness that counts."

Married women usually didn't have jobs, and they both knew it. Most men felt that a woman's place was in the home, period. They thought it made them look weak if their wives had to hire out. Sometimes an experienced schoolteacher could even be fired for getting married. Al wasn't like that, though.

"I just like to be busy. I like to be out among people. And besides, it would be nice to have a little income of my own."

"Now, May, you know that whatever is mine is yours."

"Oh, you've made that generously clear, dear. I just want to have a bit to invest, is all. With two incomes, we could do a lot more."

"You're right about that. Every day I watch those new mines up Canyon Creek. They're growing by leaps and bounds. It wouldn't hurt to be ready."

"I read in the *Free Press* that the hotel is looking for someone to cook and manage the dining room."

"There you go. You're the best cook in Idaho Territory. And you've certainly proved yourself when it comes to managing an eatery." Al looked over at her. "Are you getting too cold?"

"No, I'm all right if you are. Tomorrow I'll walk down to the hotel to see about it. There probably aren't too many folks applying. This town is nearly all miners and merchants."

"I don't care if there were a hundred people applying. You're the right one for the job." Al spoke with conviction. "No one can cook like you, May. No one."

He took her arm as they crossed the slippery street, stepping over the frozen grooves made by heavy wagon wheels. She lifted her skirt with her other hand to keep it out of the mess the horses left behind. They'd better hurry if they were going to get home by dark. That was one thing about Wallace that took some getting used to. The mountains rose so abruptly around it that the winter sun rose late and set early. It was cold down here in this crack of a canyon. Good thing she and Al were young and sturdy. Lots of folks were getting sick from the chill.

So far, the snowfall hadn't been too bad in town, but the mountaintops, according to the prospectors, were buried under drifts so deep a horse could get lost in them. Without a pair of snowshoes or skis, a man would sink to his shoulders or deeper. Sometimes May wondered if an avalanche could rumble down the slopes and wipe out the cabin. A lot of good it did to worry, though. There wasn't a single thing she could do about it.

"Here we go." Al paused in front of a store window loaded with merchandise. May gazed at the cast-iron skillets, coffee grinders, gray wool caps, and even a child's sled. "I'd like to buy you a Christmas gift. It's only two days away, you know. Tell me what you'd like." He turned to look at her and brushed a wisp of hair from her eyes.

She smiled and squeezed his arm. The warm blue scarf she'd secretly crocheted for him was already tied up with string and hidden in the cabin.

"I'll like any gift from you, honey. But since you asked, I'd love that blank scrapbook there on the left, and maybe a little bottle of glue. It's time I started keeping an account of our life together, don't you think?"

CHAPTER 14

February 25, 1888

WALLACE HOTEL DINING ROOM
Finest Eatery in the Silver Valley
Service and Cuisine Overseen By
MRS. L. W. HUTTON
Located at Cedar and Sixth Streets
Open Daily

May brushed crumbs from the hotel dining room's corner table, spread out the newspaper, and snipped around the edges of the advertisement. Imagine seeing her name in the paper! It wasn't every day a woman could read about herself in print. A man could be in the news every week, but things were different for women.

Granddad used to tell her to hitch her wagon to a star and not limit her aspirations. Society sure made that difficult. It was fine for women to keep house and care for children, but what if they wanted to do something different? Lots of people looked down their noses at working women like her, as if having a job were somehow shameful. What if she wanted to be a doctor or a lawyer or run for office—or simply vote for the politicians who would make the laws? Nowhere in the country, with the exception of Wyoming Territory, could a woman even vote.

May tucked the clipping into the little volume of Shakespeare in her dress pocket. When she got home, she'd glue it into her new scrapbook.

She'd been thinking lately about the time she'd taken Granddad to the town square to hear a political speaker, a handsome young lawyer named William McKinley. The man spoke to a small crowd gathered in the Ohio summer shade. May was probably about ten or eleven. When her legs got tired from standing, she sat down in the dust and watched a stream of ants scurry by. But when Mr. McKinley commenced talking about women and how they should have equal rights with men, she stood up again, and her legs weren't tired anymore. Just think of being as free as a boy to come and go, to attend school, to become whatever grabbed your fancy! Afterward, Granddad had invited Mr. McKinley to come home for supper and stay the night with them, as he sometimes did with politicians. As May served up fried ham, cider, and the doughnuts she had just learned to make, she listened to their talk. Women ought to have the right to vote, they'd said. It stuck with a young girl, that kind of idea.

Right now, though, it was time to get ready for her supper customers. May folded the newspaper, brushed away more crumbs, and scrutinized the room. The plank floor was swept clean and the chairs all matched. Each round table was covered with what passed for a white tablecloth with corners that hung in points nearly to the floor. Hurricane lanterns made practical centerpieces on long, dark winter evenings. The windows, flanked by heavy green drapes, overlooked the downtown street. It was as nice as things could get in a remote place like Wallace.

Those glorious words in the newspaper—"Service and Cuisine Overseen by Mrs. L. W. Hutton"—made it sound as though she dressed in finery and lolled around all day, when she was really chief cook, waitress, and bottle washer. Old Bill, who worked in the kitchen, was pretty unreliable. Sometimes he showed up and put in a full day's work, cooking and scrubbing up a storm; other times he was cozied up to a bottle and never came in at all. Today he was in the kitchen, puttering with the dinner chores.

"Bill, honey, did you remember to put the coffee on?"

"Yes, ma'am. Coffee's on, and the taters are ready, too."

"Good. After supper, I'll need you to pluck those chickens for tomorrow. And would you make sure we've got enough butter? It's nearly time to get some more from Gus."

Later, after the customers—a better-dressed, wealthier crowd than she had served at her diner—had eaten their fill and gone home, May closed the drapes, blew out the lanterns, and said goodnight to Bill. Al would be here soon to walk her home; he came for her every night, even though she assured him that she could manage the short distance alone. She parted the heavy drapes and peered into the blackness. There he was now, trudging down the sidewalk with his hands in his pockets for warmth. Her Al, who insisted that the streets of Wallace were no place for a lady after dark. She always felt buoyant walking home next to him, even if her feet ached.

"How was your day?" he greeted her, as she tucked her gloved hand under his elbow.

She leaned over and pecked his cheek in the dark. "Fine and dandy. We had a nice crowd for both dinner and supper. How was yours?"

"Kind of a bearcat. That canyon collects more snow than anyplace I've ever seen. It was tough getting through again."

"It'll be a lot easier when spring gets here."

"Everyone's saying the snow should melt off soon. It's hard to believe, though." It was nearly March, but their breath still froze in little white clouds. Underfoot, packed snow on the boardwalk had turned to ice.

"It's good of you to come for me every night." She took a better grip on his arm. With her other hand, she clutched her long skirt and tried to see where she was placing her feet. There was no moonlight—nothing but faint stars twinkling in the clear black sky.

"I wouldn't miss it. I couldn't stand to have you walk home alone." Al pulled his arm close to his chest, trapping her hand there. "It just wouldn't be right."

When they reached the cabin, Al readied himself for bed as May leafed through her scrapbook until she found the next blank page. In the dim lantern light, she dabbed glue on the back of the newspaper clipping and stuck it down, then smoothed her hand over the page and closed the cover.

Pulling on a warm shawl, she made her way to the ice-cold privy and hurried back to wash her face and hands with the hot water Al had poured for her in the washbasin. Then she undressed by the stove, slipped her long white nightgown over her head, and shook her hair down. Shivering, she carried the lantern to the bedside stand, blew out the flame, and crawled under the quilts beside Al. He reached out for her and she nestled into his warm arms.

CHAPTER 15

Al Hutton – Spring 1888

Being married to May was downright fun. She loved nothing better than to grab his hand and haul him out to one event or another. Even in this little outpost carved from the forest, there were ball games, dances, and barbecues. May wanted to do it all. He felt himself perk up whenever she let her enthusiasm loose, even when he was dead tired after wrestling the locomotive all day.

Her favorite was a handcar picnic. Sometimes on a Sunday he'd borrow a railroad handcar while May made up a basket dinner. They'd find another couple or two to go along. Then they'd all pile onto the small, open car, and with a little muscle power—the men pumping the lever, the ladies enjoying the ride—they'd go flying down the tracks looking for a good spot to spend the day. Last time, they'd made it all the way to the Cataldo Mission, ten miles west of Wardner Junction. How good it felt to get out in the spring sunshine and sit on that grassy knoll with a big spread of food.

Nothing was lacking in his life nowadays, except a bit more silver in his pocket. Their little home was as cozy as only May could make it, and he liked his job with the Northern Pacific. Of course, there were a few shadows related to his work. Labor unions were catching on here, and even though he agreed they were a good idea, they sure stirred things up and caused a lot of commotion. Maybe the hard feelings between the union and nonunion workers outweighed the benefits. He could see the day when there might be a real war between the two. It would be a shame if the goodwill in this peaceful Silver Valley disappeared.

There wasn't much he could do about it, though, except try to stay away from the tempers that flared. He liked things peaceful and quiet. May, though, she loved a good argument and wasn't shy about stating her opinion loud and clear. She'd defend the miners and their fledgling unions tooth and nail if it came down to it. He had to hand it to her; she sure had courage and loyalty. Helping the underdog ran in her blood.

Another thing nagged at him, too. Mining was getting to be big business here. By now, the larger mines were owned by corporations from all over the country. They wanted profits, just like anyone else, but their way of going about it involved investors and managers and bankers. It wasn't every man for himself like it used to be. Those earlier times, when anyone had a fair chance of striking it rich with his own gold pan or sluice box, were gone. A few years ago, with a placer operation and a dose of determination, a man could find enough treasure—usually gold—to make his way in the world. Now the whole thing was complicated with hydraulics, stamp mills, railroads, and far-off bigwigs demanding a return on their investments. And May was right; the mine owners did seem indifferent to their workers' troubles.

They were making a mess of Canyon Creek and the narrow gulch to Burke. He saw it from the locomotive every day. Tons of gravel tailings spilled out of the mountains and spewed in all directions like the guts from a dead animal. The creek found new channels where it could, but its water was pure muck. Even the trees from the mountainsides were gone, hacked down for railroad ties and mine supports. That was partly why it was so tough to get the train up the eight miles to Burke in winter. Without the stabilizing effect of the trees, snow slides roared down those nude slopes and ended up on the narrow canyon floor, right across the railroad tracks. It took the crew days of digging to open the line again.

The Northern Pacific paid him a decent wage—$150 a month—but it sure wasn't going to make him rich. Even with May's frugality and her income from the hotel dining room, it wasn't always easy to set aside a dollar or two to invest. He hoped he could adequately support a family when he and May began having children. The thought of his offspring being poor sent a shudder up his back. He'd seen enough of that in his own growing-up days.

Sometimes he got ribbed about May and her job. Just last week, a loudmouthed miner asked him who wore the trousers in the Hutton household. There had been a few jabs about keeping his wife in line, too. He silenced them with an icy stare.

Right now, though, the good far outweighed the bad in his life. May was like a rollicking gust of mountain air that had come rushing into his solitary existence and blown away the boredom and loneliness. Whatever else happened, he had May.

CHAPTER 16

August 1889

MAY STOOD ON THE BOARDWALK AND WATCHED AL EASE THE LOCOMOTIVE into town. She loved the concentration on his face as he drove the hissing black engine through Wallace, blowing the whistle and leaning from the cab to watch for careless pedestrians. Al had rigged the whistle with a chime so it gave a unique toot. His engineer's cap sat at a jaunty angle, and he waved to a group of men clustered outside the saloon. Even from the boardwalk, May could see the soot on his face. She put her hands over her ears as the shrieking locomotive drew closer.

Harry Day and Fred Harper were coming toward her, laughing and slapping each other on the back. Each wore dirty gray pants, heavy shirts, and scuffed boots. Fred's disheveled hair was strewn with bits of twigs and leaves. Both men had intelligent faces and lean builds. Harry, the younger of the two, tossed his dingy hat into the air and caught it again, twirling it on his finger like a schoolboy. Fred carried an old shovel with a weathered wooden handle.

"Howdy there, Miss Mame!" Fred sang out. They'd begun calling her "Miss Mame" when they took their meals at the boardinghouse back at Wardner Junction. It didn't matter that now she was a married woman—the name was hers forever, she guessed.

"Howdy, men. You both look like you've swallowed canaries."

"You bet! We just staked new claims!" Fred grinned. "We've got 'em all marked off and official."

"Since it's official, I guess that means I can ask where they are." May's eyes bored straight into Fred's. She could feel her heart beat faster. Maybe this was what she'd been waiting for.

Fred seemed eager to share the news. Of the two, he was more likely to talk. Harry was quiet and reserved. Both men spent part of their time prospecting, but Harry had an inclination toward business and enterprise. His father, Henry L. Day, was a respected freighter, lumberman, and road builder in the Coeur d'Alenes.

"Excuse my French, but they're way the hell and gone up Burke Canyon," Fred replied. "Perched on that steep mountain above Burke. The place was covered in thick brush until last summer, when a lightning fire burned everything to the ground. We'd never have found the mineral rock otherwise. As it is, we aren't sure if it's a solid find or not, but we aim to find out."

"I'd like to see it sometime," May said.

"No offense to you, Miss Mame, but I doubt you could climb up there. It's one of the steepest mountainsides around, and the claims are almost at the ridgeline. The slopes are slippery and rocky, too. It's rough country."

"I guess a person could ride Al's train to Burke and take the old Murrayville pack trail to the ridge," Harry put in. "Then you could bushwhack from there. But there's not much to see at this point. Just some axe blazes on burned tree trunks and a few holes. Lots of soot, too—even the rock is charred."

"What'll you call the claims?" May loved to hear the colorful names men chose for the mines. The Tiger, the Poorman, and the Frisco all crowded themselves into the canyon where Al navigated the narrow-gauge tracks along the creek.

"I called one 'The Firefly' on account of the fire that helped us find it. And Harry here called the other one 'The Hercules.' After that Greek hero, I suppose, but he saw the name on a dynamite box." Fred winked. "Let's hope it becomes a giant among giants."

May made her voice sound businesslike. "If you men think you'll need investors, let me know. I'd need to talk to Al, of course, but we might be able to buy some interests when you're ready."

"It's too early to know if these claims will even pan out, Miss Mame," Fred responded. "But we'll remember your offer. We're not about to approach any nosy corporations about investing. Harry and I, we want to use local backers if we end up needing them. And sure, we're in high spirits about our find, but do you recall Harry's old Deadwood Gulch claim? Turned out to be worthless. Harry says he'll keep on clerking and bookkeeping for the time being, just to be safe. We'll work the claims when we can."

May saw Al step from the locomotive and dust himself off. Then he turned and saw her, waved, and started walking toward them.

"Here's Al now," May said, and the men turned to greet him. "These two are celebrating, honey! They've each staked a new claim and think they might need investors someday. I told them we're interested."

Al shook hands and removed his cap. "What's this? New claims?"

"Yeah. We're cautious but hopeful." Fred rubbed his wrist, where there was a jagged cut still oozing blood. "They're near the upper end of your run—high on the mountainside above Burke."

"Way up there? They say those slopes are beyond the area that's supposed to show deposits."

"Right. Take a look at these samples, though. They look mighty promising." Fred dug in his pocket and produced some glossy fragments. He watched Al turn them over and study them. "Right now the hillside is just a scattering of stained rock with little streaks of quartz in it. We might have stumbled on something big—or nothing at all. Harry and I wanted to stake claims until we can find out. What do you think?"

"They look good to me. What do others say?"

"Pa thinks they might be something," Harry said. "He says it may be low grade, but useful. The problem will be getting to it. It's way the heck up there."

"If it's good ore, that problem will solve itself," Al replied. "There are ways."

"Yep, that's what Pa says. We'll start work on it right away, but it'll be slow going. For now, it'll just be the two of us. If we hit something bigger, we'll need investors. We'll sure keep you in mind for that. Never can tell what's up there."

CHAPTER 17

July 1890

MAY STOOD ON THE PORCH WITH A WET HANKY PRESSED TO HER NOSE, peering through the choking blue smoke. Al was down in Wallace someplace, along with every other man in the valley, struggling to put out this wretched fire. Swirling clouds of smoke billowed into the sky, while roaring flames leaped from building to wooden building. In the sunset's crimson light, May could see the charred remains of the bank, the newspaper office, the lodging house, and the livery stable. Now, through the thick haze, it looked as if the hotel were going up in flames. Men scurried everywhere, lugging kegs of water, beating at the blaze with wet rugs, and desperately shoveling fire lines between buildings. She could hear their muffled shouts and the whinnies of frightened horses.

Tears ran down her cheeks.

The houses down below were gone. Scenes from earlier in the day replayed in her mind. She'd hurried to the depot to help panicked mothers and their squalling children clamber onto the westbound train to escape the oncoming flames. Later, as May raced for home, she saw dogs streaking through the streets and people hastily digging holes to bury precious belongings for safekeeping. Overlooking tonight's scene from her porch, May wiped her wet cheeks with the hanky, grieving for friends who would return to Wallace tomorrow to find their homes burned to ashes.

She drew a shuddering breath. This was no time to be a ninny. She'd better start packing. If the wind shifted and the fire started up these dry slopes, it would race straight for their mountainside cabin. It was gusting in the other direction for now, but May knew that could change any second.

She was scared, plain and simple. This valley was a trap if the western escape route was cut off. To the east, the high pass to Montana was harsh and risky. Down in this little bowl, with mountains all around like huge walls, the best a cornered person could do was lie down in the creek and hope not to burn up. Being alone on this tinderbox of a hillside wasn't her idea of safety either.

She went into the cabin, lighted the lantern, and began stuffing their valuables into her old wicker basket and Al's valise. The money purse. Her scrapbook. The precious scraps of paper proving the interests they'd bought in various mines. A change of clothes for each of them. She topped the basket with a wrapped loaf of bread and crammed her favorite flowered hat on her head. Then she stepped onto the front stoop.

In the growing darkness, bright flames leaped and sparked and turned the clouds of smoke a rosy orange. Piles of debris smoldered red. The men were black silhouettes darting here and there. From what May could see, their efforts were in vain. Wallace was burning to the ground, and that was that. She wondered what had started the blaze—maybe someone's oil lamp left too near a curtain, or a spark from a kitchen stove.

Plenty of men down there would need a place to stay tonight. She set the glowing lantern carefully on the windowsill. Everyone knew what that meant. As long as their place still stood, the Huttons would house and feed anyone. Good thing she'd baked bread.

She would wait up for Al if it took all night. Unwanted images crowded into her mind: a burning timber collapsing on his head, a flaming wall trapping him, his clothes catching fire. She forced herself to quit imagining the worst. It was time to get busy protecting the cabin and preparing for an onslaught of hungry men. May lugged the washtub to the brook and filled it. A person could wet down the outside walls and low eaves pretty well with some sopping flour sacks.

It was midnight by the time May dragged the rocking chair onto the porch and sat soberly in the darkness. From her vantage point, the men looked like busy ants having little effect. Most were still working furiously, but a few just leaned heavily on their shovels, staring at smoldering heaps that were the remains of the general store, saloons, and "Dad" Reeve's barbershop. The stumps and brush that had been piled in the alleyways were now just angry flames. She couldn't see the hotel at all.

If the hotel was gone, her job was gone, too. May scrubbed her hands over her face. She knew that others had lost much more than just a job. Still, she loved that simple dining room and its faithful customers. And she had to admit she was keen on the extra money. It wasn't much, but it gave Al and her a little sum to invest. At least Al's job was secure, even if the pay wasn't great.

She wondered if Wallace would shrivel up and die, or if people would rebuild. She guessed they'd rebuild. After all, it was the core of the mining country, nestled here in this valley. There were new mines scattered everywhere from Mullan to Burke to Wardner Junction, up every creek and spilling out of the mountainsides. More and more people were swarming into the area, lured by the promise of silver and gold.

May's head nodded. When she jerked awake again, the flames looked smaller, and they had quit leaping from building to building. Quite possibly there were no buildings left. She couldn't tell for sure through the smoke. A large crowd of silhouetted men had gathered in the main street, and someone was speaking.

She rose and went inside. As she was making a crock of cold tea, she heard voices outside. The door opened. Al walked in, followed by a bunch of others. His face was streaked with sweat and soot, and his clothes were black. His heavy boots left footprints across the floor.

"Oh, Al, you're safe!" May rushed to him and Al's arms went around her, knocking her hat to the floor.

They didn't speak for a moment. Then Al said, "Didn't do much good down there. Pretty much everything's gone." His eyes were bloodshot. "I told these fellas they could sleep here, and maybe you'd give them something to eat. The boardinghouse burned up."

"There's room for everybody if we squeeze," May answered, retrieving her hat and grabbing the tin cups to fill with tea. "Is there anybody else who needs a place to stay?"

"Not tonight." Al's hand trembled as he took a long drink. "Gus, help me move the table out of the way. You and Fred and Harry can stretch out on the floor here. A couple of you others can sleep on the front stoop, and there's room for two more by the stove."

May looked around at the exhausted men with their somber faces. Along with Gus, Fred, and Harry, there were five others, already removing their boots.

"In a minute I'll get you some blankets," May said briskly as she started around with slices of crusty bread. You'll have to share, but you're all so tired you're going to sleep like logs. I'll stay awake and make sure the wind doesn't come up again."

CHAPTER 18

July 1890

"Harry, this plateful's for you, and these are for Fred and Gus." Morning sunlight poured in the window as May's eyes swept over the men crowded into her little house. Still covered in sweat and soot, they leaned against the walls, squatted on the front-room floor, and sprawled in the mismatched chairs. "Al, pour more tea, will you, while I slice another loaf of bread?"

May could feel the color high in her cheeks, and her hair, stuffed into a bun, coming loose. She hadn't slept, but instead had spent the night pacing between sleeping bodies and keeping watch for stray flames. Glancing down ruefully at the same wrinkled dress and apron she'd worn yesterday, she fetched another loaf and began slicing. The men had awakened early, despite their exhaustion, and needed breakfast. After the disaster last night, she was scared to start a fire in the stove to make coffee, but everyone seemed happy with the cold tea.

There wasn't much conversation today, just glum silence. The men stared into space or rubbed their sooty eyes.

In the morning light, May could see that Wallace was almost gone. The hotel was nothing but a black, smoldering pile of debris. Al caught her staring and put his arm around her shoulder. After a moment, he said, "We sure did try to save it, honey."

"I know you did." They stood there for a minute, watching the smoke rise and drift away. May turned back to the kitchen.

Harry stopped chewing, cleared his throat, and stood up. He stepped to the center of the room, onto the big multicolored braided rug May had made from rags.

"Men, here's what we've got to do." His booming voice filled the cabin. The others looked up from their plates. Even in his creased, filthy clothes, Harry somehow had a refined look about him. He surveyed the room with a direct gaze. "We will go down there and rebuild the town! This time we'll use bricks. We'll ship 'em in from Spokane or Missoula, and make our buildings so strong and fireproof this town will last for the next hundred years."

Several of the men cheered. May let out a whoop. "That's the way, Harry!"

Fred put his half-empty cup on the floor and sat up straighter. "This place is prone to fires. Think about all the lightning fires we've seen on the mountains. We never would have discovered the Firefly and Hercules if the brush hadn't burned away. I agree. It doesn't make sense to rebuild with lumber."

Gus, his mouth full of crusty bread, nodded. "We need to rebuild fast. The mines depend on having a town here, and it'll be hard times until we can re-establish things. The sooner, the better, I say."

"Me, too," said Dad Reeves. His gray manicured beard was smudged with ashes. "I guess I could give haircuts in a tent for now, though."

"I think I'll just move on down the road and go to work for the Wardelena Mine," a skinny young man piped up from the corner. "They're hiring."

There was silence. May looked over at him as she stood by the table, spreading the last slices of bread with butter. She'd seen him a few times in town but until last night hadn't known his name. Todd Belknap. He barely had whiskers yet, and his face seemed so young that May wondered where his mother was. His unkempt hair stuck out in all directions and hung below his dirty collar.

"You be careful of that Wardelena Mine. They don't treat their workers right, in my book," May began. Al put a hand on her shoulder. "Are you ready to work seven days a week, ten hours a day, at that shameful wage they pay?"

"Well, ma'am, at least there's a company boardinghouse to live in."

"Sonny, you listen to me. The Wardelena is no place for the likes of you. There are too many ways to get yourself hurt, or killed, or maimed for life. What if you fell from those high timbers in the dark? Or how'd you like to be trapped in there in a fire? I could go on all day."

"Now, May," Al put in. "The boy's just trying to find himself a new job and a place to stay."

"Well, the Wardelena's not it! It's a dreadful place, in my opinion. And it's not the only one. I don't think any of those mine owners care a whit if someone gets hurt or killed—they just hire a new man to replace him."

Gus wiped his mouth on his sleeve. "Those big companies are so worried about profit that they don't think about the workers. They've ruined things here with their big-city ways and investors and noisy equipment." He ran his fingers through his bushy blond beard. "A man who just wants to work a little claim hardly stands a chance anymore."

"Nowadays, hired miners are expected to work for peanuts." May's voice rose. "Meanwhile, our friends and neighbors breathe that horrid dust until their lungs are full of it—and put up with getting sick and hurt or even killed." Boy, oh boy, she could get steamed about mining conditions.

"Folks, we're talking about rebuilding Wallace here." Harry smoothly changed the subject. "I'm going down to clear Pa's plot and see where we can get a shipment of bricks. Anyone who wants a job laying brick for us can have it. Belknap? How about it? Want to lay some brick?" He handed his empty plate and cup to May. "Thank you for the lodging and breakfast."

"Think nothing of it, Harry. Anybody who needs a place to stay again tonight is welcome to come on back."

The others rose, thanked her, and trickled out the door. Al stood on the porch seeing them off and making sure they had a supper invitation. Todd stayed behind. "Do you really think the big mines are all that bad, Mrs. Hutton?"

"Yes, I absolutely do. Gus is right: All they think about is the almighty dollar. If a miner gets hurt, there's no help for him at all. And, heck, it's awful dangerous down there. You listen to the miners sometime. They'll tell you about balancing their way across high timbers with nothing below but a big black shaft. Not even a handrail. Or about blasting their eardrums out with the noise of dynamite, and coughing all night from the dust. Others say that rattlesnakes hide down there and the lighting is so bad you can't even see where you're putting your feet. One fella told me he fainted from the heat once, and his buddy barely caught him before he fell into a vertical shaft. They work 'em so long and hard they can't see straight. I tell you, Todd, it's not a place you want to be."

"You think laying brick would be better?"

"I sure do! And working for Harry and his Pa would be better, too. You want to stay here with Al and me until you can build another cabin?"

"Well, thank you, Mrs. Hutton. Maybe for a night or two until I can put up a lean-to or find a tent to pitch. Heck, it's July, so camping should be fine."

"All right. But you be sure to take your meals here until you get your feet on the ground. Go catch Harry and tell him you'd like to be a bricklayer. He'll show you what to do and he'll pay you just fine."

CHAPTER 19

Autumn 1890

MAY TOOK A SIP OF LUKEWARM COFFEE. SHE'D MOVED HER ROCKING chair onto the shaded porch for these sunny fall days and was working on a new winter shirt for Al. Setting the black sleeves into the armholes was taking forever, and there were still the buttonholes, the stiff collar, and the hemming left to do. She rubbed the back of her neck. Maybe she'd put it aside for today and work on her writing instead. She sipped her coffee again and looked out over Wallace. Another forest fire must be smoldering somewhere far away, because the air was hazy. Shafts of pale yellow sunlight washed over the town.

It was amazing how quickly those handsome brick buildings were going up. Wallace was beginning to take shape again, and this time there were none of those drab wooden structures. Gone were the flimsy false fronts with tiny windows that looked like beady eyes peeking out of a broad face. This time, thanks to bank loans and a few investors willing to go out on a limb, solid brick buildings rose two stories above the straight streets. One even had a marvelous bay window that stuck out over the walkway below. In the autumn sunsets, the orange brick glowed from the new downtown until it seemed to warm the entire valley, and the windows reflected the golden light.

There weren't any dining rooms to manage—or anyplace else to work—in town yet. Time would take care of that, but it wouldn't do to be idle, so May baked and sold huckleberry pies for extra income. And she began writing to fill the hours. She loved stringing words together, one after another on a page. They made sense when she was done, and all that practice was making her better at it. Best of all, since no one read them, she could be as blunt and unguarded as she wanted—hell, use every colorful word in the book!—and people wouldn't cluck their tongues or roll their eyes. Writing down what mattered made her feel good. She denounced the bad treatment the miners got and attacked the mine owners, all in her most scathing words. By now, the table was littered with pages and pages scrawled out with her black fountain pen. Al kept her supplied with paper.

Sometimes she sent a letter home to her half-brother Lyman and the rest of the family. When she worked out here on the porch, shielded from the sun by its crude roof, the warm mountain air smelled like cottonwood and pine. Little breezes swished through the boughs overhead with a soft whispering sound. Woodpeckers tapped on the fragrant bark while she worked, flitting silently from tree to tree. Maybe she should write a poem about this place.

She was still reading everything she could get her hands on, too. The new words she came across seeped into her brain and became a part of her. Folks were generous about sharing their books, so she had a sporadic supply of leather-bound classics, dime novels, and everything in between. What this town really needed, though, was a library—a place where people could borrow books for free and read to their hearts' content.

Just as she decided to fetch her pen and paper, she glanced again at the valley and saw Al stride from behind the buildings. He began climbing the lane toward home. What in the world? It was far too early for him to be off work. As he got closer, she could tell that his pipe was clenched in his teeth—the pipe he usually reserved for relaxing in the front room after dinner or leaning back in his comfortable chair at the Masons' meetings.

He stomped onto the porch, his face flushed and his eyes snapping. He grabbed the pipe from his mouth and held onto it, white knuckled, while he ran his other hand through his hair.

"Those hooligans! They just can't settle this peacefully!"

May knew instantly what he was talking about. The conflict between the union miners and mine owners was on everyone's mind. The folks who found their way to the Hutton cabin for visits had many a heated discussion about it right here on this porch.

"The new unions are doing their job, but not without stirring up a hornet's nest," Al steamed. "Up there in Burke today—and in Gem, too—the mine owners are saying they can't afford the new railroad shipping rates. The workers are afraid the owners will close the mines to make the railroads bring the rates down. If that happens, hundreds of men will be out of work. I tell you, May, the miners are finally getting organized into unions, but they were so worked up this afternoon that I was honestly afraid they'd riot. I got the train out of there fast and called it quits for the day."

May stopped rocking. She'd never seen Al so riled. Imagine him defying the schedule and bringing the train home to Wallace so early in the day!

"Al, honey, here's my rocker. Just sit for a minute." She scrambled to her feet.

"I tell you, there's going to be a war in that canyon!" Al sat down and puffed nervously on his pipe. May noticed he'd forgotten the tobacco. "Those poor miners are scared."

"They should be! What would happen to all those families if there were no work? It's shameful of the owners even to suggest such a thing! Maybe the miners should strike and show those big shots a thing or two."

"They'd just bring in strikebreakers."

May moved behind the rocking chair and rubbed Al's shoulders. She felt his muscles relax. His heavy shirt was soaked with sweat, and she pulled the collar away from his hot neck, blowing on his skin to cool him. Al was silent for a few minutes. He pulled his tobacco pouch from his pocket and sat fingering it. When he spoke, his voice was calmer. "I'll probably catch heck tomorrow for quitting early, too."

"You can tell them you were just protecting the train. That's the truth. They ought to be glad."

"They'll dock my pay a few hours. It's hard enough to make ends meet without losing pay."

"Don't you worry about that. We'll make do," May soothed.

"I guess so. But don't forget, May: If the mines are closed, there'll be no need for a train engineer, either."

CHAPTER 20

Al Hutton – July 11, 1892

He leaned from the locomotive's side window and gaped at the crowd swarming to climb aboard the train. Even in the moonlight, he could see it was nearly all wild-eyed and disheveled women. A few clutched valises or blanketed babies. Others were fumbling with their hair, hurriedly stuffing it under hats. The children with them were crying or sucking their thumbs, hanging onto their mothers' skirts. Al had never known there were so many families squeezed into Canyon Creek gulch. Sometimes he'd caught sight of a lady or two pushing a stroller or sweeping dirt off her front stoop, but apparently Burke, Gem, and Frisco had a whole population he'd never seen. And now it was up to him to get them out of here. Fast.

"Climb aboard, ladies, quickly!" he shouted. The engine's huffing and hissing almost drowned out his voice. "Let's get out of here!"

He watched the Gem Mine warily as he waited for the last woman to help her little girl onto the only passenger car. The moonlight illuminated a makeshift barricade across its entrance. He could see the gleam of gun barrels poking through its holes. Behind it, he was sure, was a crowd of hired guards and nonunion workers. Across the street, Daxon's Saloon was ominously quiet, even though it was filled to the brim with union miners. A gunfight could break out any minute. Taking a deep breath, he opened the throttle and the engine lurched forward.

His heart hammered as the locomotive charged down the track, shattering the night's stillness. It was just what he had predicted: warfare in the gulch. He could only imagine what was going on farther up the canyon. He'd overheard angry threats yesterday about blowing up the Frisco Mine with dynamite but had figured they were just boasts. A while ago, though, an explosion up the gulch had rocked the entire canyon.

The mine owners had sure asked for it, though. During the past winter, they had closed the mines. Workers and their families were victims of the fight between the railroads and the owners over freight costs. The families had hunkered down, trying to survive the deep snows and cold temperatures without income. If it hadn't been for some generous farmers over in Palouse country who sent food, there would have been real starvation. Al, too, had been out of work part of that time; he and May had lived on the meager income from her pies.

The final blow came in the spring. The owners said they would open the mines, but only if the workers put in longer days—some up to seventy hours a week—at the same pay as before. The union men refused. That was when trainloads of strikebreakers started showing up. Union workers responded by meeting the trains with guns, forcing the newcomers to go back home. Then the owners hired armed guards, who also met the trains and escorted their new employees to work.

It was a powder keg, pure and simple. And Al was right in the thick of it. The only way he had survived so far was to stick to his work and keep his mouth shut. Whether he wanted to or not, it was part of his job to carry men on both sides of the issue up and down the tracks. The union guys tried to talk him out of transporting strikebreakers and nonunion men. "C'mon, Hutton," they'd say. "If you're not helping the union, you're hurting it." But he had to stay out of it as much as he could.

His hands were steadier now at the controls. He took a few deep breaths and thought of May. She'd been awakened, too, when the messenger banged on the cabin door at midnight and breathlessly told Al he was needed to rescue the women from Burke and Gem. She was probably waiting up for him, pacing the floor until she saw the locomotive's bright headlight pull safely into Wallace.

May defended the unions to anyone who would listen. In fact, she'd been writing down her views on the issue. He had read a few of her handwritten pages. She could really put her thoughts on paper. Sometimes he was alarmed at how forthright she was with her opinions, but he guessed nobody would ever read her scribblings but him.

He rubbed his eyes. Boy, he was tired. He didn't feel sleepy, though. Just kind of sick to his stomach and jittery. No doubt he'd find out in the morning how many men were dead in Burke. And probably Gem, too.

He sounded the whistle as he pulled the train into Wallace. The ladies and children were safe now. He would help his shaken passengers disembark and then go get May. She'd want to come to the platform and find places for these poor, red-eyed women and their youngsters to spend what remained of the night. He knew several of them would end up at the Hutton cabin, spread out on the floor under every one of May's quilts.

CHAPTER 21

July 12, 1892

MAY COULD HARDLY BELIEVE HER EYES WHEN SHE SCANNED THE HEAD-
line story in the *Free Press*. The rumors were true, then: The union men
had blasted the Frisco Mine's concentrator into kindling wood. Miners
had sneaked to the top of its water flue, drained it, and used it to send a
load of dynamite hurtling into the mill. On top of that, there had been
a gun battle at Gem. No one was sure yet how many men had been hurt
or killed.

May had walked all the way to town to get this morning's newspaper.
Now she was trudging home, reading as she went. It was a clear, sunny
day and already hot. She adjusted her hat and paused in the shade of the
new White & Bender building to read the news more carefully.

Federal troops had been ordered to the Coeur d'Alenes to restore
order. They were on their way. In the meantime, the armed union miners
had left the deadly chaos at Frisco and Gem and stormed into Wardner.
There, they seized some of the outbuildings at the Bunker Hill and Sullivan mines and threatened to dynamite them to smithereens like the
Frisco Mine if the troops came close, or the strikebreakers didn't leave.
Apparently the company saw no choice but to shut down and evacuate.
Astounding. May reread the lines. It was a David and Goliath story like
no other.

While she secretly rejoiced at the union's success, mostly she was sobered. Men were dead up at Frisco and Gem. Even with order restored, the rift would remain.

May fanned herself with the newspaper before starting up the lane to home. Usually she noticed the mountain maple, elderberry, and wild rosebushes partly shading the way and filling the summer air with their fragrances, but this time she trudged along without lifting her eyes.

Al wasn't working today. The Northern Pacific wanted the train to stay put, safely in Wallace. It would take time to clear the dynamited debris from the tracks anyhow. Maybe tomorrow he'd be able to return all the scattered women of Frisco and Gem to their homes—or maybe they would just have to walk home when they felt it was safe.

By the time she reached the cabin, she was out of breath and her light cotton dress was damp with sweat. Al was gone, but the three women who had spent the night on her floor with their children were gathered on the porch.

May's heart went out to them. They were young and upset by the violence, of course. One, an intelligent girl in her early twenties named Martha, told May that the unrest had been brewing for days. She'd spent the last frightening evening huddled under her quilt with her four-month-old baby. Another, a blonde woman with a nervous laugh, said she'd forbidden her children to play outside for the week preceding the Frisco event. That's how tense things had been. She was sure her cabin windows had been blown out by the blast.

"The trouble is, this doesn't solve a thing," she lamented. "Here we are, seven miles from home, imposing on a perfect stranger, while they're locking our men in the schoolhouse. And the concentrator is gone!"

May started to answer when one of the toddlers, a sweet-natured child named Laura, pinched her finger in the door and let out a howl. May swooped down, folded the startled little girl into her arms, and held her tight. Then she carefully handed her to her mother and stepped back. The child smelled so clean, and her delicate fingers had curled around May's so unexpectedly. May watched as the toddler buried her soft face in her mother's neck.

"I'll bet your men will be released soon," May answered slowly, her eyes still on the child. "They can't put the whole mob in jail, and most of 'em weren't involved in the violence. I think you'll be all right. But remember, you can stay here for as long as you want."

That night, lying awake in bed beside Al, May could hear the soft breathing of the children sleeping on the kitchen floor. Normally, she would be stewing over the disastrous events of the day, but tonight she couldn't stop thinking about holding little Laura. May was taken aback by the yearning she'd felt when she held the child. For a long time after she and Al were married, she had hoped that they would have babies. She hadn't quite given up. Maybe someday she would wake up pregnant. But it should have happened long before now. Al had mentioned it wistfully once, too, although he generally kept quiet. May knew how much he loved children.

It was several days before the women from Frisco felt it was safe to return home. They caught a ride with Al when he returned to his regular route. May went with them to the station, making sure each had a fresh loaf of homemade bread wrapped in a clean cloth tucked in her bag.

As they climbed aboard the train, May was struck by how vulnerable they looked. Their faces were peaked as they waved good-bye and the train pulled out of the station. Watching them, May thought about how unfair life was for women. Those young mothers were smart and capable, but the way things were here in Idaho Territory, they had almost no control over their own lives—no voice at all in the political process that ruled them and their children. It was a shame, that's what it was. Somebody should do something about it.

CHAPTER 22

July 1892

THOSE WOMEN FROM FRISCO SURE DID PUT A BEE IN HER BONNET; IT had been buzzing there for a couple of weeks. Every time she thought about how women in mining country—and almost everywhere else, for that matter—had no say over the laws imposed on their lives, she started to burn up. Why was it that men got to make all the decisions—and women had to live by them? May fumed as she grabbed the old kitchen bucket and headed to the creek for water.

Whenever she found a cause she felt strongly about, she got a burning in her chest that seemed like fire. That's just how she was. The more she thought about it, the more it smoldered until she decided what action to take. Then the burning turned into tireless energy. She could work day and night on an issue like miners' rights if she thought some good would come of it.

Her zeal for women's rights was like that. She paused in the shade of a towering white pine and leaned against its trunk. Ever since old Granddad had told her to hitch her wagon to a star, May knew she wanted women to have the right to vote. She closed her eyes for a minute, imagining equality. If women could vote, things would be better. Here in Wallace, they could bring about progress like schools and hospitals and the right to own property.

A sudden thought occurred to her and her pulse quickened: If she wanted equality, she'd have to see to it herself. Hell, all those men out there weren't going to make it happen. They were so used to women playing second fiddle that they barely noticed it was wrong.

She started walking, her thoughts spinning. She was dying to meet the women who were fired up about women's rights in the West. She would seek them out. In this day and age of train travel, it wouldn't be hard. She'd save up enough for the fare to Boise or maybe Idaho Falls. Al wouldn't mind. He always supported her. Think of all the young girls and babies whose lives would be better if there were equal suffrage in Idaho!

May had heard of a newspaperwoman from Portland, Abigail Scott Duniway, who was in Idaho now, working for women's rights. It was people like her May wanted to meet.

She reached the creek. It wasn't the roaring stream that it was in April, when melting snow created a boisterous near-waterfall here. Instead, it had settled into a mild brook happily burbling down the mountainside to the larger creek below. May held the bucket by the handle and stepped onto the flat rock Al had placed on its bank so she could scoop water without muddying her shoes. Not that a little mud bothered her, but it was just like Al to think of it.

She filled the bucket, set it down, and settled herself onto the rock, pulling off her scuffed shoes and stockings. The water felt like ice on her feet. Overhead, the pines were quiet and still in the afternoon heat. She could smell their fragrant bark and the carpet of fallen needles warmed by the sun. She sat for a while, letting the current tug at her legs, and then leaned forward, pulled up her sleeves, and scooped water over her hot face and arms. Yesterday, she'd even poured a bucketful over her head, soaking her clothes for the short walk home. Good thing no one was around. Imagine how the fine ladies of Wallace would talk about that! May didn't care if she looked like a drowned rat with cascading water turning her hair stringy and dousing her pink gingham. She was cool and refreshed; that was what mattered.

Those ladies didn't understand her. She didn't understand them, either. How could they ignore the unfairness of the world, the tangle of social injustice and prejudice and inequality? It was impossible for her to be close friends with such women, to whom Saturday teas were more important than votes for all. Surely they must notice that women were treated like second-class citizens! Couldn't they see the plight of the common miner? No one could live here and not be aware of the long hours, the illnesses, the deadly accidents. Heck, she would be ashamed of herself if she sat calmly on the sidelines, fretting over silly tea parties without fighting for what was right.

Her face and arms dried in the dappled sunlight. May pulled on her stockings and shoes with new purpose. She would write a letter to Abigail Scott Duniway, offering her services for the cause of suffrage. The miners needed her help, too, so she wouldn't put their issues aside. But she had time for more than one worthy cause.

May stood and grabbed the bucket. Water sloshed over her shoes, but she barely noticed as she turned to hurry along the trail, stopping now and then to switch hands when the heavy load made her arm ache. She could begin working for suffrage here in Wallace while she waited for Mrs. Duniway to answer her letter. Maybe she would start by announcing she wanted to vote in the next election. That would make a few men sit up and take notice!

She'd vote for good male politicians if she had to—but someday maybe there would be women running for office, too. Heck, maybe she'd run herself.

PART II
FOUR YEARS LATER
1896–1903

CHAPTER 23

November 30, 1896

Howdy, brother Lyman,

It's been a heck of a long time since I've written, but I'm still alive and kicking out here in good old Wallace. I'm sitting here at our kitchen table keeping an eye on my clean laundry (frozen stiff!) hanging on the clothesline out back. There's a pesky squirrel that likes to nibble through the rope until my whole batch of washing falls in the snow.

This morning, the heat from the woodstove feels good on my back. Winter has set in, and somehow it feels colder down in this deep canyon of ours.

Al is still driving the locomotive for the Northern Pacific and I've been working for women's suffrage here in Idaho. I've spent my time scurrying all over our new state, sometimes with Abigail Scott Duniway, a suffragist I met from Portland. She was as determined as I that Idaho women should have the vote. We lectured and campaigned until we nearly dropped, but I'm proud to say we carried the day. Not long ago, I voted in my first election!

Of course William Jennings Bryan got my support.

Wallace is still having labor clashes. The mine owners keep hiring nonunion workers, no matter what the unions do. Al tries to avoid the conflicts as he engineers the train, but it is impossible for me to stay neutral. I'll fight to my dying day for the unions. The men here are finally organized, thanks to a few strong leaders and the Western Federation of Miners. I won't go into the issues here, but will just say that the troubles are not over. Every so often, a fistfight or worse, a gunfight, breaks out, confirming the tension that constantly simmers under the surface in these parts.

Idaho is a rough place, not that it bothers me any. The West opens its arms to all the things the East tries to cull out: prostitution, shootouts, cussing, and such. That's partly what makes life so interesting. Even though the repeal of the Sherman Silver Purchase Act caused the end of the silver boom (that's why we needed William Jennings Bryan as our president), things change by the minute here. In the nine years Al and I have been in Wallace, we've watched this place turn from an ugly mining camp into a little city. Despite the tight times, we've got electric lights downtown now and even telephone service if you're rich enough to afford it. Al, bless his heart, likes to take me to all the baseball games, lodge socials, and picnics. A few weeks ago, there was a play put on by some actors from Spokane, and we all went, dressed in our best.

Layoffs are so common here that the men expect them. Most of our friends have been hurt by the dive in silver prices, but they're sticking it out. They've done some serious tunneling at the Hercules Mine, for instance, with just enough good results to keep them working. I don't know how much longer they can hold on without some backing money.

As for me, I've been doing fine. While Al is moving ore cars between Burke and Wallace, I find more than enough to keep me busy. I spend my time writing letters by the dozens, mostly to politicians about fair labor and equal suffrage. (The suffrage work is not done, because Washington and Oregon still linger in the Dark Ages. Women cannot vote there—yet.) In between, I bake and sell my famous pies, read books, and have been thinking about writing a novel. I'm glad I came to the mining district and wouldn't change my decision for anything.

I hope everything is fine back home. Send me a letter! The post office here is good, along with the other services we have in Wallace now—there's even a theater and a photography shop. Our cabin overlooks them all, perched as it is on the hillside above town. I love to wake up in the mornings to the raucous call of the magpies that swoop through the pines. Sometimes I leave treats for them and the chickadees outside the window. Even the squirrel that chews my clothesline gets a little snack now and then. I can't hold a grudge when he's so captivating.

Give my love to all, especially little Daisy. But I guess she isn't so little anymore.

May

CHAPTER 24

September 1897

MAY WAS WASHING THE BREAKFAST DISHES WHEN THERE WAS A KNOCK on the cabin's door. She dried her hands on her apron and hurried to open it. Friends often dropped in, but it was too early on Sunday morning for that. Al was out back stuffing rags in the cabin's leakiest cracks.

Harry Day stood there with his hands in his coat pockets. He was dressed in the tough canvas pants men wore while digging their claims. His friendly face was serious and his thin hair, already receding at the hairline, was uncombed. Beside him was Dad Reeves, who had purchased Fred Harper's portion of the Hercules-Firefly diggings when Fred got discouraged by the slow progress. He, too, wore dark pants and a heavy gray shirt.

"Howdy, fellas! C'mon in! The coffeepot's on." May held the door open. "Let me get Al."

In a moment, the four of them were settled near the stove sipping May's strong coffee. Harry sat forward in the rocker with his feet planted on the braided rug and his elbows on his knees. May and Al looked at him expectantly, but it was Dad who cleared his throat and said, "Folks, this is a business call."

Harry's eyes traveled from Al's face to May's and back again. "We're here to see if you're still interested in investing in the Hercules."

"It's about time you asked!" May blurted. "How long has it been since you and Fred staked your claims? Eight years, isn't it?"

Al said cautiously, "Why don't you tell us what you have in mind."

Dad took a sip from his steaming cup while Harry continued. "You're right, Miss Mame. Eight years. Sometimes it seems like a hundred. But we're convinced there's something worth pursuing up there. I've invested almost a decade digging by hand and inspecting every inch of the way. The thing is, the two of us can't hold on much longer. We need capital."

"There are some other local folks we're going to approach as possible investors, too," Dad added. "No big corporations, though."

May glanced at Al. His piercing eyes were trained on Harry's face. "How much do you need?"

"We figure we can continue if we sell interests to you folks, Gus Paulsen, and that new fellow, Harry Orchard. Gus says he'll put down some of his savings and work full-time at the prospect hole for a quarter of the holdings. We're asking you two to put down $505 for one sixteenth."

"Whoa! That's a huge chunk of our savings, Harry." A furrow appeared between Al's eyes. "What makes you think you're going to strike it big?"

May started to speak, but thought better of it. Al would come around. She knew he would. He just needed time to think it over.

"I don't believe you'd be sorry, Al. Look at the other mines up there. They've been producing for years. They're lower in the gulch, but there's enough richness in the Hercules rock to make us think there could be a big vein somewhere close. It's just going to take perseverance and a little money to find it."

"If anyone has perseverance, it's you and Gus," Al said slowly.

"That's right. If we add investment money, we can make progress. Al, maybe you could help with the assessments, too. We have to assess our progress and labor every year according to the mining laws." Harry leaned back in the rocker. Behind him, a log in the woodstove settled with a soft thud.

"I think Fred was hasty in selling his interest to me," Dad said. "But I'm glad he did. I have a feeling about the place. It isn't named the Hercules for nothing."

"Did you bring samples?" May asked.

Dad reached into his pocket and pulled out a dirty pouch.

"Right here." He got up and poured the samples out on the table. "I dug these yesterday."

As they clustered around the table inspecting the dusty rocks, Al glanced at May. She knew what he was thinking. After all, they'd been married for ten years. He didn't want her to blurt out a commitment here and now. He wanted to digest the idea, weigh the pros and cons, and come to a reasoned decision. That wasn't her style at all, but she respected it in Al. She herself liked to follow the feeling in her gut. She made decisions based on information, yes, but also on her strongest hunches. This time, her hunch was screaming at her to go ahead. What were she and Al waiting for? Five hundred dollars was a lot of money—a lot of huckleberry pies and pennies pinched over the years—but no one was getting rich with it timidly stored in the bank.

"We'll talk this over and let you know in the morning," Al said. "Right, May?"

She sighed. "That's fine, honey. Can we reserve our spot until morning, Harry?"

"You bet, Miss Mame. If you decide to come in with us, take the money to Dad at the barbershop first thing in the morning. We'll put it to good use, I assure you."

CHAPTER 25

September 1897

MAY CLOSED THE DOOR BEHIND HARRY AND DAD, BUT THEN OPENED IT again. No use shutting out the autumn sunshine. Soon enough it would be blowing snow. She refilled Al's coffee cup and sat down at the table with him. Silently, they fingered the rock samples. Al rubbed his temples and looked up at May.

"I know you want to go in with them," he said. "I do, too. I just need to think things through."

"We can't get the money from the bank until morning anyhow," May answered.

"Are you ready to risk everything on this? Think how many years it's taken us to save up five hundred dollars."

"I'm more than ready. This might be our big chance."

"It could be just another dead end, too." Al took a sip of his coffee.

"It could. But the Hercules is right there in the canyon where all those other mines are doing fine. Gus and Harry are good, solid men. Dad, too. I'd trust 'em with my life."

"They're dependable, that's for sure. Gus has shown more determination than anyone else in these parts. But what if we spend our savings on the Hercules and then something better comes along?"

"It could happen. Think how many years we've been buying little interests and provisioning grubstakers without much to show for it, though."

Al stood up, went to the window, and looked out over the valley. May went and stood beside him. She took his hand in hers. "Whatever happens, honey—even if we lose it all—we'll still have each other."

He kissed her cheek. "I'll have to spend my days off at the prospect hole, digging and mucking out, or figuring the assessments."

May winked. "I'll just come along and dig, too."

Al smiled. "You'd do it, too! They've built a shelter at the mouth of the hole. It's not much, but it's out of the weather. There are hundreds of feet of hand-dug tunnels by now. Let's go up there and take a look, shall we? I'll borrow a couple of horses."

"Do you think my backside can stand the trip? It's about eight miles each way, isn't it?"

"I'll find you a nice gentle mare."

"All right. Give me a few minutes to make up a picnic."

Al met her at the depot an hour later with two horses from the livery stable. May handed him the wicker basket and hoisted herself into the saddle from a bench on the boardwalk. She hadn't been on a horse for a while; hopefully this one was surefooted and gentle. Al swung himself up easily, and they turned toward Burke.

The well-traveled road left Wallace and meandered up Canyon Creek. Undergrowth shone gold in the late September sun under a deep blue sky. The scenery up here probably used to be stunning, but now the creek was muddy from the mining upstream. Big piles of tailings spilled out of gashes on the mountainsides. The road and the railroad tracks made twin scars as they competed for space in the narrow canyon.

They reached Burke before noon and began the steep trek to the Hercules. May leaned forward in the saddle and held on. She hoped the old mare wouldn't stumble on the rocky trail. The horse swayed beneath her, climbing steadily and lurching over big stones and tree roots.

By the time they reached the diggings, May was famished. Oddly enough, no one was there. She and Al sat on a ledge eating chunks of crusty bread with sharp cheese while overlooking the canyon. They had gained a lot of altitude, and it felt to May as if they were perched on the edge of the world. Far below, Canyon Creek tumbled down the gulch. Cabins and mines were scattered across the mountainsides. A hawk glided on the updrafts. May tried to get a glimpse of Wallace but couldn't see it because of the way the canyon curved. Nearby, diggings from the Hercules were dumped down the slope. A crudely built log cabin stood at the mouth of the tunnel with tar paper tacked haphazardly over its roof.

When they finished eating, Al grabbed May's hand and helped her to her feet. They entered the cabin, feeling like intruders, and stepped into the cold, damp entrance tunnel. The mine snaked its way into the mountainside and disappeared in utter blackness. May blinked. It was gloomier than heck in here. The air smelled like dust. She couldn't imagine how anyone could see a thing once they got beyond the light from the opening. Harry and Dad and the others used candles or lanterns to make their way deep into the hole, but it seemed to her that those tiny sources of light would be completely swallowed by the void. She reached for Al's hand. They stood for a moment in the dank air, peering into the mountainside.

"It's sure timbered up nicely," Al commented.

As they stepped from the prospect hole back into the windowless cabin, their eyes had finally adjusted to the darkness. This time they could see the picks, shovels, and candle stubs that littered the floor around a makeshift table, and old tin cans from past meals tossed into a back corner. May knew she could whip this place into shape and make it a fine little kitchen. Add a cookstove and a few pots and pans, and she'd be ready to turn out meals for Al and Harry and Gus. She'd cooked in worse places.

They lighted the stub of an old candle and ventured into the hole again, this time going deeper. May ran her hand over the walls and noted spidery veins of ore in the rock. Al sneezed from the dust; the sound echoed in the tunnel. May laughed and let out a couple of loud hollers just to hear her voice bounce back. Then they turned around, blinking as they emerged into the bright sunlight and grateful for the fresh air. Al wandered across the mountainside above and below the hole, kicking rocks and parting undergrowth and sifting through the tailings pile. Then he joined May on a warm, flat boulder.

"I'm no expert, but it looks good to me, May. Harry thinks there's potential here, and I'll bet he's right. It might take a long time to find out for sure, though."

"I say we're in. I can get the money from the bank tomorrow morning and deliver it to Dad."

"Good. If nothing else, we'll have a shot at making our fortune."

CHAPTER 26

December 1898

Four months had passed since they invested in the Hercules. Despite weeks of hard digging, there had been no rich discoveries, just more dirt and rock. May sighed as she stared out the cabin window at the gathering darkness.

Downtown Wallace twinkled with electric lights, and the lodge was ablaze with lamps in preparation for tonight's ball. Darkness came early now that it was December. The snow had taken on its pretty cobalt color, signaling the end of the day. Al loaded the woodstove and turned down the damper to keep the place warm for the evening. May picked up the wicker basket filled with buttery popcorn balls and found her gloves.

"Are you ready, honey?"

"Just give me a moment to get my coat."

May looked at herself in the oval mirror Al had fastened to the wall. Her color was high and her hair swept up, curling from under an emerald-green hat. The hat matched her dress—the one she'd made for occasions like this. She liked the way the wool skirt fell in folds to her toes. The dress was warm, which was welcome on a bitterly cold night like this. It looked nice, but hadn't cost much, even after she added the sparkling false-diamond buttons down the front. She'd made sure of that. The recession and the dip in silver prices had affected Al's income. People back East called this decade "the gay nineties," but life hadn't been so optimistic for folks in mining country.

Al was pulling on his coat and making sure he had his gloves. The years had begun to etch faint lines around his eyes, but May thought they only made him more handsome. He was trim, and his dark hair was as thick and wavy as ever. Her heart always gave a little leap when he dressed up like this in a white shirt and black jacket. She still couldn't believe she was married to him.

Al's gloves, she noticed, had a hole in the finger. She must remember to darn it for him so they wouldn't have to buy a new pair. As he shut the cabin door, she took his arm, and they stepped off the porch. The lane was deep in snow. May lifted her skirts, thankful she was wearing her boots and carrying her dress shoes in a string bag. Even so, the icy coldness found its way through her stockings as she and Al pushed through the knee-high drifts. Around them, the dark pines sagged under the weight.

Al carried the basket and the little gifts they would tie onto the branches of the Masons' Christmas tree—a hand-tatted doily for a woman and a black picture frame for a man. Lots of folks were getting their pictures taken these days.

May was chilled by the time they arrived at the lodge. She and Al stomped the snow from their feet and sized up the gathering crowd. Nearly everyone was there, dressed in their best Christmas finery. They were all talking at once, and the din was pierced by raucous laughter. In the back of the big hall, long tables were covered with food. For once, May hadn't brought a main dish or a pie, but had decided instead on these new molasses and butter popcorn balls. She'd read they were all the rage in big cities.

"Well, well, if it isn't the Huttons." Harry Orchard stepped forward to greet them as May pulled off her boots and put on her shoes. He tipped his hat at May and shook Al's hand. Harry was the other new partner in the Hercules, along with Gus. May thought it was odd that—of the thousands of men's names in the world—two of the mine owners were named Harry. Harry Day and Harry Orchard. There was a fundamental difference between the two, though. Where Harry Day had quiet charisma and understated leadership, Harry Orchard was, in May's opinion, just plain bold.

"How're you doing?" Al spoke loudly above the commotion.

"I'm full of hope, Al. Full of hope. I don't see how the mine can fail. It's simply a matter of time before we investors will be dancing in the streets."

"We're going to have to put in a hell of a lot of hard work before that happens," May commented. "That ore doesn't just leap out of the ground."

Harry winked at her. He was a big man with a high, shiny forehead and a charming smile. The buttons on his coat strained over his stomach, and his eyes roved the room as he talked. There was something about him that May didn't like. Maybe he was too cocky— or too smooth. Nevertheless, she and Al were in business with him. Al would do a better job of keeping things congenial. She took the wicker basket and went to find a place on the buffet tables for the popcorn balls.

Sweeping across the crowded room, May called out to everyone she knew. Some of the men hollered back, and most of the women greeted her warmly. A few averted their eyes, though, or skittered into the kitchen to avoid her.

After a while, she and Al joined a table with other couples whose plates were piled high. Across the room, the Christmas tree was laden with gifts everyone had tied to its branches. The overhead electric lights made the room as bright as day. Nellie Stockbridge, the new assistant photographer in town, had set up her camera in the corner and was busy taking photographs. Rumor had it that she'd been professionally trained in Chicago. May settled herself between Al and Gus, exchanging greetings with the others at the table. She was glad her voice was so loud; it certainly helped her be heard in a crowd like this.

After supper, the tables were moved aside and the dancing began. The piano and violin duet in the corner was warming up with Christmas carols. This was the best part of the evening, as far as May was concerned. There was the added benefit of being held in Al's arms for as long as each song lasted. Once, as they wove their way near some newcomers, Mr. and Mrs. Mulroney, she called out a greeting, but the well-dressed couple turned their backs and danced in the opposite direction.

"That's a fine way to treat people," May grumbled in Al's ear.

"Both of them together can't hold a candle to you," Al answered and held her tighter.

May sighed. Al was so good at staying calm. She relaxed in his arms and let him guide her around the floor. The sounds of *Silent Night* filled the room. She could dance with Al until dawn, if only her feet weren't starting to hurt.

CHAPTER 27

February 1899

MAY TOSSED THE DIRTY DISHWATER OUT THE BACK DOOR AND WATCHED it melt a hole in the new snow. Last night's storm had piled another foot on top of the already deep drifts. The cabin was nearly buried in the heaps that slid from the roof and hid the windows. Al had to shovel the trail to the privy every day in this weather.

May lifted her eyes to the treetops and took a deep breath of the crisp air. She sure was tired of being cooped up. The Christmas dance seemed like years ago. There hadn't been any social events since then; everyone was too busy surviving winter. Chopping wood. Clearing paths and roads. Hacking through ice to get to the creek for water.

She and Al were as good as snowed in. Yesterday, Al had ventured to town for some camaraderie and a newspaper, but May hadn't wanted to slog through the drifts to get there—and then struggle her way back. She could sure use a change of scene, though. The cabin was clean and cozy, but the four walls were shrinking closer every day. She had a good case of cabin fever, she guessed.

Whenever the walls closed in, she would step outside and soak up the stillness of the wintery woods. Even though she complained about the white drifts that kept her homebound, there was nothing as beautiful. A deep hush settled over the mountainside, muting the sounds from town and filling her with peace. She'd draw in a lungful of fresh air and marvel at the snow's subtle scent. When the wood smoke drifted the other direction, she could smell it—a distinct, fallen-from-the-sky aroma there were no words to describe. She'd bend and touch her toes a few times to get the blood flowing, and then arch her back to study the dark-green branches above, laden with snow, bending toward the ground. The drifts were pink in the morning light, deep blue in the fading evening, and, on rare sunny days, full of sparkling diamonds that twinkled and shone in every color.

May liked the cold weather, but it sure made life more difficult. If only the winters weren't so long. She still had a bruise on her hip where she'd fallen on the path to the privy last week. That must have been a sight. Good thing no one saw her floundering in the snow, trying to get up. And getting water was such a chore she'd taken to melting icicles from the eaves instead.

Today, she could smell the smoke from Al's pipe as it floated out the open door, and the venison stew that bubbled on the stovetop. She'd left the door open to air the place out and get rid of the stale odors and fumes from the lamp.

At least she and Al got along famously, even when he was home all day. The tracks had to be cleared again before he could run the train. She'd heard of couples who fought so badly they couldn't last the winter holed up together. Sooner or later, one of them would bolt—the man to the saloons, the woman to a friend's. She and Al had an occasional spat, maybe once a season or so, but it was never anything serious. How could she ever stay irritated at her Al, the most endearing creature on this earth? Besides, she liked having him home. He was good company. Plus, it kept him away from the trouble that was brewing here like a vat of whiskey. Things were getting more and more volatile. May was afraid Al would get pulled into the mess whether he wanted to or not. She worried about him, out there with the rough-and-tumble miners every day. No telling what those fellows would do if they were pushed far enough. Oh, she had plenty of sympathy for their cause! But plenty of worry for Al, too.

She sighed and went back indoors. At least she was getting a lot of reading done while the weather held her captive. She'd borrowed a copy of *Romeo and Juliet* from the new shopkeeper who shared her interest, and was slowly making her way through it. That Shakespeare chap was sure tough to follow, but if she read his work line by line, it was like eating from a box of chocolates. It was astounding, really. The man had been dead for almost three hundred years, yet his words still resounded. She wondered if he had ever imagined that a snowed-in woman in the Idaho wilderness would spend her time memorizing his lines.

Shakespeare inspired her to write: poetry in her own down-home words, straight-shooting letters to government bigwigs, notes back home, and the full-steam-ahead beginning of a novel. She wanted to write about life here in the Silver Valley, and the *issues*—to strike back at those who didn't treat the miners right. There were enough colorful characters right in Wallace and Wardner to make a whole book, especially if she disguised them by changing their names. She wouldn't disguise their flaws, though. Maybe she'd work on it again today.

Al interrupted her thoughts. "Did you know that Gus is up at the Hercules, digging away, even in this weather?"

"What? He has to be crazy!"

"Last time I saw him in town, he told me it's warmer underground than it is outside, and the dirt is only frozen on the surface. Deep underneath, it's just like any other day."

"How does he even get up there with the snow so deep?"

"I think he's staying there. He's taken up enough food to last awhile and just sleeps in the cabin. There's plenty of firewood."

"Well, if he isn't the most persistent fellow I've ever known."

"Yep. Faithful, too."

"It must get awful lonesome up there."

"Terrible. Gus can handle it, though. He's got one thing on his mind, and that's to dig until he finds something. Something big."

CHAPTER 28

Al Hutton – April 29, 1899

He froze at the locomotive's controls as a cold gun barrel pressed into his ribs. Someone behind him—he couldn't see who—choked off his air with a huge hand around his neck.

"You'll be all right, Hutton," a man's voice growled in his ear. "Just do what I say."

Al's heart pounded as he tried to get a good breath. Whoever it was stank of tobacco and whiskey, and here it was early morning.

"Better let me breathe then," Al managed. He clutched the controls to steady himself.

The hand loosened its grip, but the gun stayed where it was. "Stop this thing at the Frisco and stay there until I say."

"Take that gun away."

"Shut up, Hutton. Do what I tell you." But the gun no longer pushed against his ribs. "You're taking us down to Wardner Junction. Lots of us."

Al turned his head slightly, but he couldn't get a look at whoever was holding him captive. He didn't recognize the voice, either. Maybe if he knew who it was, he could talk his way out of this. From the corner of his eye, he could see a second gunman aiming a sawed-off rifle at the train's fireman.

"You fellas want to go to jail?" Al's mouth was dry.

"Shut up, I said."

"Because that's where you'll be when the sheriff comes."

"Hutton, you hear me? We're not worried about that puny sheriff. He'll be so outnumbered, he won't dare try anything smart."

It was true. As the train rounded the curve, Al could see a crowd of men pushing and shoving beside the tracks—a couple hundred of them. In the gray morning light, they looked like a bunch of cutthroats with their caps pulled low over their eyes. Some wore masks. Others had put on their Sunday clothes, as if this were a holiday. Most had fashioned white arm bands, probably from their wives' flour sacks. Someone stood on a stump, shouting and gesturing. Al blew the whistle to warn them to move back.

"Damn it, Hutton, don't blast that thing again," the gunman barked. "We can't draw attention to ourselves."

Al brought the train to a shuddering stop. The crowd swarmed aboard, while a few of the men muscled crates of dynamite onto the last car.

Dynamite. Lots of it.

Wardner Junction had been a festering sore among the union men for a long time because the Bunker Hill and Sullivan reportedly hired non-union workers at a lower wage. The management was said to have fired some fellows just because they joined the union. Al had heard talk about blowing the place to smithereens just like the Frisco Mine back in '92.

He wanted no part of this. People could get hurt or killed again. He set the brake and tried to make a break for the door.

Immediately, the gun jabbed him in the ribs again. "Don't try it, Hutton."

There wasn't much he could do with that gun ready to blow him apart. These men were so riled they wouldn't listen to reason. Still, reason was all he had.

"If you boys are planning on blowing up that mine, don't think you won't get caught," he tried. "And if someone gets killed, it could mean getting locked up for the rest of your life."

"Enough of your preaching, Hutton. Just take us to Wardner Junction." Al felt the gun push harder into his back. He lurched the train into movement. There was no stopping these hooligans now. They'd want him to halt in every town along the way to pick up more men until he had an overflowing trainload of them. They meant business. That much dynamite could do the job.

He swallowed. His hands ached from his white-knuckled grip on the controls, and he was sweating as if it were August. Outlandish ideas about how to escape whirled through his head—jumping from the moving train, tackling his kidnapper, taking the wrong tracks. Any of those would probably get him killed, though. He knew he had just one choice if he was going to get out of this nightmare alive. He'd have to do what they said. By the time the train was full, there could be almost a thousand men aboard. Then he'd have to take them to Wardner Junction. He'd be forced to break all the rules, even go the wrong way on tracks that didn't belong to the Northern Pacific.

He hoped he didn't get shot or fired or both.

Maybe he could blast the whistle again to alert the sheriff. But there was no telling what that bad-tempered gunman would do. Besides, what could one lone lawman do to stop a whole trainload of armed hellions bound for revenge?

Already some were riding on top of the train cars brandishing their guns. The locomotive's chugging and hissing drowned out their voices, but he could see they were loaded up with liquor.

He took a deep breath. Whiskey and dynamite and the morning's bound-for-glory mood were a bad combination.

CHAPTER 29

May 29, 1899

MAY KNELT IN THE DIRT AND FISHED IN HER POCKET FOR THE PUMPKIN seeds. Her garden spot was covered with dead pine needles again, even though she had raked it yesterday. A breeze rippled the long sleeves of her work shirt; she pushed them up to feel the sun on her skin. It was warm here against the back wall of the cabin. The soil sifting through her fingers smelled like springtime—damp and musty, with a promise of things to come. The ladies in town wore gloves for gardening, but May loved to feel the dirt's grittiness, and break up the clods with her bare fingers. She began digging a little hole for a seed when she heard running footsteps on the front stoop and loud knocking.

"Mrs. Hutton, are you here?"

May shoved herself to her feet, barely noticing the pain in her knees, and headed around front. Young Todd Belknap was waiting impatiently by the front door.

"What's wrong, Todd? You're all red in the face." She wondered if he'd run all the way from town. The last time she'd seen him, he'd been laying bricks for Harry.

"Mr. Hutton's been arrested and locked up. He's in the bull pen!"

May couldn't believe her ears. Her Al! Held captive with that trainload of enraged men who blew the Bunker Hill and Sullivan's expensive mill to pieces. Locked up with the rest of them in that huge stockade-like structure people called the bull pen.

"No! Are you sure, Todd?"

"Yes, ma'am. Them soldiers, they rounded up all the miners—and Mr. Hutton, too."

Two men had been killed by the dynamite blasts. That meant big trouble. But how could they possibly pin blame on Al? He'd been forced at gunpoint to drive the train. A few high-ranking people were going to hear about *that*.

She needed to see him. May glanced at the low sun. It was too late today to make it to the bull pen and back before dark. She'd wash up, eat supper, and set out to see Al in the morning.

In the early morning light, she could see a small city of white tents laid out in neat rows below, housing federal troops. Governor Steunenberg had asked President McKinley to instigate martial law after the Bunker Hill and Sullivan incident. Some of the tents were big and round with cone-shaped tops that came to a peak in the center. Others were small and rect-angular, like tiny houses placed cheek to jowl in a muddy field. They gave things a somber feeling. Soldiers were climbing out of the canvas doorways, stretching, and tying their boots.

The newspaper said it was against the law to approach the bull pen, but how else was she going to talk to Al? She circled around the back. The win-dowless walls looked plenty thick and solid. With a quick glance around, she hitched up her skirts and climbed through the barbed-wire fence. Tall, rough-hewn boards rose high above her head to meet the pitched plank roof. Good thing there were plenty of knotholes. She found the biggest one and peered through. It was dark inside, but May could make out men mill-ing about on the dirt floor and sitting on hard wooden bunks. There weren't any guards back here. Maybe they figured no one could get out of such a place. It looked like its name—a big, locked-up pen for animals.

"Pssst." May caught the attention of the nearest man inside. "Bring Al Hutton over here, would you?"

There was silence. May tried again. "You know, the train engineer. I'm his wife."

The man moved away, and pretty soon Al peeked through the knot-hole at her. There was enough room to slide her forefinger in and touch his unshaven face.

"Honey! Are you all right?"

"Yes. You're going to get in trouble, though. No one's supposed to come near this place."

"Just let them catch me. I'll give them a piece of my mind."

"I've been fired, May."

"Fired!"

"Worse than that, they're trying to point the finger at me. They claim I didn't try hard enough to stop these hoodlums from their dynamite spree, and that I should have done something to keep the train from being mobbed."

"With a gun at your back? That's ridiculous! Isn't the Northern Pacific glad you kept the train in one piece? It could have been you and the train that got blown up."

"They don't see it that way. I told 'em about the guns and dynamite. But I used the train for an unlawful trip. And I had to take some risks. Driving the wrong direction on non-company tracks was the biggest one. Not that I had much choice."

"You had no choice at all! How dare they think any of this was your fault? Have they ever had a gun stuck in their ribs?"

"There's no reasoning with them."

"They'll rehire you once this is over. They'd better."

"They seemed pretty set on letting me go."

"I want you out of this place. Here, I brought some warm socks and a pair of gloves. It must be damp in there. I think I can poke them through this hole one at a time. Anything else you need?"

"Well, there's not enough food."

"I'll smuggle in something nice."

"The fellas in here are pretty upset. A few of them are talking about trying to kick up another storm. But mostly they're good men. They're worried about their families. What's done is done, though. That concentrator looks like a bunch of toothpicks strewn across the hillside."

"What did they expect? But I'll get you out, honey. You just watch. I'll write the governor and anyone else who'll listen. I'll raise such a ruckus that they'll let you go just to get rid of me."

"Now don't do anything rash, May. I'd be glad to get out, though."

"Don't you worry. And I'll be back tomorrow with something to eat."

Her cheeks were flushed as she trudged home. Hell, she'd send letters to any newspaper that would publish them. She had a way with words—and the gumption to follow through with action. She'd tell it exactly like it was and hammer out the ways Al was innocent. Then she'd harass the politicians, everyone from the governor on down. She'd get the Masons working on this, too. Al was well-liked in his lodge.

May stopped at the butcher shop to pick up a nice, plump chicken. She was thinking about the best way to smuggle it into the bull pen when the door opened and Nellie Stockbridge walked in. May often saw her around town toting her heavy camera equipment.

May liked the looks of her. Miss Stockbridge was a trim young woman who was intent on her profession. She wore a plain black dress—neat and clean but definitely serviceable—and her hair was drawn into a secure knot under a plain hat. Her long face was edged by a fringe of tightly curled bangs, and she had dark eyebrows over a long, straight nose. She was pleasant in a no-nonsense way. May wondered if she was sympathetic to suffrage. There weren't many professional women in Wallace. They must feel the need for equal opportunity. She'd ask sometime, but today there was something more urgent on her mind.

"Miss Stockbridge, have you been down to the bull pen with your camera? It's going to be in the news, I can tell you."

"As a matter of fact, my employer, Mr. Barnard, and I did get some photographs of it in the evening light the other day, both inside and out. They're still in negative form; I haven't had time yet to print them."

"My Al is in there, you know, and he's innocent."

Nellie looked straight into her eyes. "I've heard. You must be troubled by that."

"You can bet your life I'm going to do something about it, too," May pledged as she put the wrapped chicken into her canvas bag. "That's how I know the bull pen will be in the news. I'll make sure it is."

CHAPTER 30

May 31, 1899

As MAY CUT UP THE RAW CHICKEN IN HER SUNNY KITCHEN, THE REALITY that Al had been fired hit her. There would be no income other than her pie money, which wouldn't begin to support them. If the Northern Pacific didn't rehire him, she and Al would be in a real pickle. The other railroad probably didn't have an opening for an engineer, and if they did, they certainly wouldn't take the NP's castoff. She paused, her knife in the air. Al could go to work in the big mines, but he'd do that over her dead body. She didn't think she could stand to see him there. Those were places where men died or got hurt regularly—or wound up coughing their way to the grave. By that time, Al would be a pauper who owed a big debt to the company store. She knew all about it.

May began hacking the chicken again with a vengeance. Al had worked hard to get where he was! He'd put in seventeen years of good service for the Northern Pacific. A good, honest man like him didn't deserve to be fired. And now he was locked up like a criminal.

The main task now was to free him from the bull pen. She dumped the chicken into her cast-iron skillet and tossed more wood into the stove. First thing tomorrow morning, she would march back to the pen and harass the guards to let her in. No more peeking through knotholes. Al needed a blanket and a nice warm coat. And she'd write her letter to the governor right now. As the chicken began to sizzle, May grabbed her pen and a new sheet of paper. This was no time to mince words; the governor would know exactly what she thought. Later on, she'd make this bull pen incident the heart of her novel. Of course, she'd invent some new names for the devils in charge of arresting Al and holding him captive. She could think of some good ones.

She didn't sleep well that night. Her heart kept pounding and waking her up. Without Al's soft breathing beside her, it was hard to go back to sleep. The stove creaked as it cooled, owls hooted in the woods, and coyotes yipped nearby. She was up at dawn, wrapping pieces of chicken in three separate cloths and burying them deep in the pockets of her blue calico dress, where they would blend with her generous curves. The guards would never suspect a thing.

She left the cabin early again, and, just as the sun was rising over the mountains, strode up to the first guard—a boy no older than sixteen, she guessed—and demanded to see her husband.

"I'm sorry, ma'am, I can't let you in there."

"You'd better, young man. My husband's locked up, and I'm not taking 'no' for an answer."

"It's orders, ma'am. No one's allowed in there, especially not any women."

"Sonny, who's your superior? Let me talk to him this minute."

"Gosh, I'm just following orders!"

"Well, this is one time to bend the rules. I know how to raise hell, believe me. Besides, who's going to know? I'll sneak in and sneak out before your commanding officer ever comes near."

"Will you make it quick, ma'am? Because I'm not supposed to . . ."

The young soldier's hands fumbled with the key as he unfastened the padlock and slid the heavy metal bolt aside. May stuck her hands in her pockets to cover the wafting aroma of fried chicken. She'd have to find a quiet corner to be alone with Al. If those locked-up men knew she had food with her, there'd be a riot for sure. She nodded at the young man as she stepped past him into the bull pen. "I'll be inside for just a few minutes today, sonny, but I'll come back tomorrow. Don't give me any problems."

He glanced furtively up and down the street. "Hurry, ma'am. If I get caught, I'll be strung up and cooked for dinner."

Al was in the exercise yard, squatting in the dirt with a handful of other men. She saw him before he looked up, and her throat closed. He looked so discouraged, sitting on his heels with the high plank wall looming behind him. His hair was uncombed. Normally he'd never allow it to stick up in back that way. The dark pants he wore were spattered with muck and bits of hay. Even his face looked gray in here. The yard was muddy from the rain earlier in the week. A terrible stink hit her nose and almost made her gag. In another corner, three men sat on their heels playing poker. Mostly, though, the large space was empty. May guessed that the rest of the prisoners were still in their crude bunks inside the barracks. Al had always been an early riser.

She called softly to him. "Al! Good morning!"

All eyes turned to her, and the men scrambled to their feet.

Al grinned. "I might have known you'd get in here somehow, May. How'd you do it?"

"Oh, I have my ways. That poor guard out there looks like he belongs in a playpen. I've got to talk to you, Al. Is there a place?"

"Nope, this is it. Maybe we can use the far corner, though. Excuse me, men."

"What's that awful smell?" May asked, as Al took her arm and steered her to the vacant spot.

"The latrine," Al replied, his mouth set in a straight line.

"Heck, honey, you're liable to get sick in this disgraceful place. I've written the governor to get you out, and I'm raising Cain with a few other folks, too."

"Thanks." Al was grim. This time he didn't caution her not to do anything rash. Instead, he raised his face to the sun and shut his eyes. "I don't know what I'll do if I can't get my job back."

May slipped a piece of the wrapped chicken into his hand. "Not the big mines, Al. I don't want you there."

He glanced around before giving her a grateful look and ravenously gnawing the meat off the drumstick. May had never seen him so hungry. She rubbed his back as he ate. A bit of color returned to his face.

"I've got some ideas about how to talk to those big shots from the NP," she said.

"It won't hurt to talk to them. But they're not going to change their minds. I can tell you that much."

CHAPTER 31

Spring 1899

IT TOOK TWO WEEKS, BUT SHE'D DONE IT.

All those letters she'd written, along with a bushel of threats and plenty of loudly persuasive visits to the Masons, had found their mark. Al was home, skinny and tired, but ecstatic to be free.

"I feel like a new man," he told her after he'd bathed in the washtub and put on clean clothes. "You can't imagine how grim and filthy it was in that place. The fellas are getting mighty tired of being cooped up. Some of 'em were pretty tense. Those officials are insisting that they drop their union memberships if they want to be released."

"That sounds illegal to me." May put her hands on her hips. "Just like all the bull pen shenanigans."

"They wanted me to make a list of who was on the train that day. I can't rat on those guys! Besides, most of 'em were masked. I couldn't see who they were anyhow. They even wore their coats inside out to hide their identities." Al peered into the mirror. His hand shook a little as he shaved the stubble from his cheeks. He left the mustache.

"The whole thing is a big mess," May answered, handing him a towel. She studied his face in the mirror. She could swear there were more creases around his eyes than there had been a few weeks ago.

Al shaved for a while longer. "I've been thinking. I should go up to the mine tomorrow. Gus could use some help tunneling. It must get discouraging for him up there, digging every day without much to show for it."

"I've thought about that, too. What would we do if he quit?"

"If Gus quit, we'd be in a bad fix."

"Maybe he could use help with the mucking, too. I'll bet he gets tired of that. I could make a fresh batch of yeast buns for you to take. He's probably sick of his own cooking."

"That'd be nice. And May, there's something else I want to tell you."

"What's that?"

"You're a gem, that's what." He set down the razor, and turned to face her. "I never doubted that you could get me out of the bull pen, and I love you for it." His hand brushed her cheek as he leaned close and kissed her softly.

She smiled. "I couldn't let you be treated that way. I'm so glad you're home, honey."

"Me, too. More than you'll ever know."

"What do you want to do today?"

"Right now, I'm going to walk downtown and thank the Masons. Then I'll be right home. Maybe you could make up a little dinner and we'll meander over to the creek with it, just the two of us. Take it easy in the sun awhile."

"That sounds nice."

She stood on the front porch and watched Al trudge down the mountain. His shirt hung loose on his bony shoulders. She'd have to fatten him up, that was all.

Packing a good picnic would be short work today. She had plenty of smoked trout and homemade pound cake to toss in her basket. The floor needed sweeping, but she'd do that later. While she waited for Al, she wanted to add a few more paragraphs to her book manuscript.

She sat at the kitchen table, where she could look out at the wildflowers. She loved those big golden daisy-like blossoms that grew in tall clusters under the pines like fallen stars. Some years, there was barely room to walk between them. The rest of the undergrowth was a vibrant spring green.

113

Her version of the Bunker Hill and Sullivan story was coming along nicely. There was satisfaction in describing real people—those mine owners, for instance—in her fiction. She was having a great time coming up with unpleasant monikers for them. She used real places, too, thinly disguised. Everyone would know exactly where she meant anyway.

May was used to hard work, but she hadn't expected writing a book to be such a struggle. It took a lot of sweat to put so many words on paper, and a lot more to get her point across. She dipped her pen in the ink and began scribbling. Fortunately, there was a perfect place in the romantic plot to squeeze in her opinions about habeas corpus and martial law. Reading over what she had written, she scratched out a word or two, rewrote a couple of sentences, and put the page with the rest of the manuscript. It was just right.

Al would be back any minute. Most men would drink and smoke all afternoon with their friends, but not Al. Even after all these years in a rough mining town, he still never drank. He'd have a quick visit with his friends at the lodge and then come home.

She had to admit she was worried about him. Always before, he'd had the railroad to keep him busy—sometimes too busy. It was demanding work, but Al had taken great satisfaction in engineering that big locomotive. He'd told her once that he loved the pure power of the massive engine and how its mighty force vibrated through his body. Being fired by the Northern Pacific was going to leave a huge hole in his life.

May tapped the end of her pen on her chin. He'd need a new direction, that was for sure. Not that Al ever floundered for long. But she would encourage him to put his time into the Hercules. The more hours he spent helping Gus, the better.

CHAPTER 32

Early Autumn 1899

AL HAD BEEN BACK AND FORTH TO THE HERCULES ALL SUMMER, WHICH gave May plenty of time to write. Most days, like today, she brewed a nice pot of coffee before she settled down by the cabin's window, where the light was good.

By now, her manuscript was a hefty pile of paper. She called this book a novel, and it was, sort of. But she'd made sure it was peppered with her own political views and as many scathing editorial remarks as she could dream up.

She knew the story meandered a bit. But then, she never claimed it was a literary work. It was a book with a purpose, set right here, smack-dab in the middle of this labor conflict. If it vilified or ridiculed certain local people, they deserved it. Besides, she'd changed their names, although that didn't really disguise their identity. So what if someone took offense and wanted to sue? She and Al didn't have two nickels to rub together, so it wouldn't do much good.

In another few weeks, the manuscript would be ready to publish. She'd painstakingly saved up enough to travel to Denver for that chore. There was a printing and engraving company there that had agreed to take her scribbled manuscript and turn it into a book. A little shiver of excitement ran up May's spine. It wouldn't be long until she could say she was a real published author.

Before she left, she'd sell as many promised copies as she could here. Wouldn't it be something if the book actually made some money? Damn, it would feel good to have enough coins in her pocketbook to enjoy some of life's niceties. It would sure help with household expenses, too, now that Al was unemployed. With the rest, she could be as generous as she wanted. Hundreds of redeeming causes ached for a few dollars. There was a lot to be done for human suffering, if only she had the means.

She'd best rein in her thoughts, though, and knuckle down to work. She blew on her coffee and took a long sip. Maybe no one would stop by the cabin to distract her today, although she relished visitors. It was a rare day when she could write without interruption. Sometimes, though, a rousing discussion with a neighbor got her blood boiling, and that made for fired-up writing afterwards. She took another sip.

She would head up to the Hercules tomorrow, taking the train to Burke and then hoofing it up that exhausting mountainside. Al would be there, and Gus. Probably that nice hired man, Ed, who helped muck out the waste rock. Not the two Harrys, though. Harry Day had to travel back and forth to Boise now that he was Secretary of the Idaho Senate. And Harry Orchard? She'd been right about him, it turned out. He was a gambler, and had to sell his portion of the Hercules to pay his debts. A few new folks bought his share: Harry Day's brothers and sister; Gus's old boss Mr. Markwell and his sons; the storekeeper at Burke; and a couple of others. They were good local people. By bringing them in, the partners had been able to keep the Hercules going without selling out to the big mining companies. Nearly every other glory hole in the area ended up doing just that. Mining was expensive, and the only sure way to keep money flowing in was to sell out. Not the Hercules, though. That would happen the day hell froze over.

May looked down at her blank sheet of paper. The words just weren't flowing today. She sighed and stood up. Grabbing the old wooden bucket, she left the cabin and climbed the mountain slope. It wouldn't take long to gather the dusky blue elderberries she needed for pies to take to the mine tomorrow. She wanted to cook the bear roast her neighbor had given her, too. If she put the meat on the stove before she went to bed, seasoned with onion, salt, and sage, it would be tender and ready to wrap up in the morning. A nice slab between thick slices of bread, along with wedges of elderberry pie, would keep the men going.

It had rained all night, and a light mist was still falling. The air was cool on May's skin; she welcomed it after the hot summer. The elderberries hung in ripe, glistening clusters. Silver droplets pooled on their leaves. A cloud clung to the mountaintops and draped into the gullies like a gray coverlet. From here, the mining gashes across the valley were hidden in fog. May could picture how this valley must have looked before the mining rush brought machinery, road scars, scalped mountainsides, and dirty towns. Beautiful.

She filled her bucket quickly. Elderberries were easier to pick than huckleberries, which grew one by one on low bushes. A woman could pick huckleberries all day and end up with barely enough for a few pies. These elderberries fell off the branches in heavy clusters, and they were already washed, too, thanks to the rain. No need to dunk them in the creek.

As she returned to the cabin, she forced her mind back to her writing. She would dedicate the book to Al, to defend his reputation for honesty and decency. It was even more important now, after he got arrested and locked up in the bull pen. What was that word she'd learned? Probity. That was it. It described Al perfectly. She hurried now, eager to write her dedication. Her mind would get ahead of her fingers, and she would have to slow her thoughts to let her pen catch up. That's how she was. She thought quickly and made headlong plunges. Set things in motion. She would finish this book, vindicate her labor friends, and show the world just how things were in the Coeur d'Alenes.

CHAPTER 33

Al Hutton – Fall 1899

He stood on the tailings pile from the Number Two Tunnel and looked out over the gulch. May should be here soon. The trip from the canyon floor to this lower level wasn't as far as it had been to the original diggings. He grabbed the side of the metal ore car and stretched his sore back. How many times had he, Gus, Dad Reeves, and their hired hand Ed Hedin filled it and dumped it over the side of the mountain? Maybe they had time for one more load before May arrived.

He turned and pushed the ore car ahead of him into the tunnel. The narrow tracks were swallowed by the blackness, despite the lantern hanging from the car's side. Good thing he'd never been shy of the dark or of confined spaces.

The partners had decided to quit the original diggings and start anew here. Harry's younger brother, Jerome, had done a crackerjack job of timbering the sill. From there, it had been sheer hard labor, day after day, month after month, to dig and shore up this second tunnel by hand.

He wished the Hercules could afford a widowmaker—a compressed air drill—instead of just hand drills. The larger mining companies all used them. They were dangerous, but they penetrated rock much faster than men working by hand. Buying one for the Hercules was financially out of the question, though. Maybe it wasn't so bad: May hated that word "widowmaker."

He paused to give his eyes a chance to adjust to the darkness. Then he gave the ore car another push, ducking his head to avoid the overhanging rocks as he followed the tunnel deeper underground. The familiar smell of damp earth rose to greet him along with the distant, echoing ring of Gus's sledgehammer.

He knew about the dangers inside a mine but didn't let himself think about it much. No use alarming yourself when there was work to be done. They had dug a smart, sound tunnel, although cave-ins were always a possibility. That was one thing that could spook a fellow—the thought of being trapped underground without air or a way out.

Boy, he was hungry, despite the huge breakfast he and Gus had wolfed down before dawn. This physical labor sure did work up his appetite. Maybe he'd look for May one more time before mucking another load. With any luck, they could break for a midday meal. He turned and made his way along the dirt floor to the tunnel entrance again.

"Halloo, honey! I'm almost there!" May's voice called from the woods beyond the nearby stumps. He caught a glimpse of her bright yellow blouse through the trees and started down the slope to meet her.

"Sorry it took me so long. This basket is pretty darn heavy." She was dressed in men's bib overalls, and her face was flushed. Folks ribbed him about his wife climbing up here and mucking, but May was strong, and every set of hands helped. He thought the overalls looked fine on her, rolled up at the cuffs and stretched over her generous hips. The yellow blouse underneath added a feminine touch. May always looked feminine to him, no matter what she wore. In the mine, she put on an old canvas hat. It became her as much as those flower-bedecked things she wore in town.

He took the basket from her and gave her a long hug. "Glad you made it safely. What's in here?"

"A couple of pies and a bear roast, plus bread and a few doughnuts for later on. Is Gus underground?"

"Yep. I was just going back in myself. I'll holler at him to come eat. Ed is in there, too."

"Wait a second and let me lay the food out. I have something to tell you, anyhow. Dad Reeves is thinking about selling part of his portion so the Hercules can bring in more local investors."

"That's decent of him. Lord knows we need more capital. Costs are going up every day. Harry's sister, Ellen, is pitching in some of her school-teaching money, but we've still got a long way to go."

"I'm glad you and I added that second lump of investment cash when we did," May replied. "And I'm glad we staked out those adjacent claims. It'd be a lot harder to do it now. Here, honey, could you drag these boards out of the shade and lay them across those logs? We'll eat in the sunshine. We can use this flour sack for a tablecloth."

The mouth of the Number Two Tunnel was strewn with debris, just like the original opening. Rubble and tailings were piled in heaps between extra logs cut to shore up the entrance. Crude low buildings roofed with tar paper provided cramped workspace and much-needed shelter from the elements. In winter, the mountain snowstorms were something awful. The snow was so deep a man had to have snowshoes just to get around. It would be easy to freeze up here without a hefty dose of common sense.

He set up a makeshift table next to a pile of supply sacks. May unwrapped a big chunk of meat and a lump of butter. She pulled a loaf of bread from her basket and began slicing and making sandwiches.

"I saved some bear grease for your cracked hands, honey. There's enough for the others, too. It's the best thing for chapping and soreness, even if it does smell bad."

"Who wants to smell bad?" He grinned.

"If you can stand me in overalls, I can stand you in bear grease. Go ahead and try some."

CHAPTER 34

Fall 1899

GUS APPEARED AT THE TUNNEL'S MOUTH, SQUINTING INTO THE SUNSHINE. Beneath his battered felt hat, his face was covered with dust. Dirt was caked to his pants, and one elbow poked through a hole in his shirtsleeve. He blew out his lantern and set it carefully on an upended stump.

"Howdy, Gus," May called out. Al stood nearby, rubbing grease into his hands.

"Howdy, May. What's this? Sandwiches?"

"It's the least I can do. Feed you, I mean, when you're working so hard up here."

Gus's eyes didn't sparkle when he talked about the mine anymore. Sometimes she noticed a faraway look on his face when he sat on the mountainside and gazed at the gulch below. Right now, his shoulders slumped as he waited for May to hand him a sandwich.

He was the best laborer of them all. Gus could keep swinging a pick long after the other men were done in. The muscles in his arms bulged after years of hard digging, and the calluses on his hands were tougher than cowhide. He had perfected a sideways pickaxe swing, too. The ceilings of the tunnel were usually too low for good overhead swinging that gave a man real power. And while some people couldn't take being underground all day, it didn't faze Gus. He didn't seem to mind the dank, chilly darkness or working alone.

"This here tunnel, she's a tough one," Gus said as he hungrily bit into the sandwich. "I wish we'd strike something, because I sure feel like a fool digging worthless holes in this hillside and hauling ore like a work-horse—all for nothing. This one's almost sixteen hundred feet deep now and there's not much to show for it."

"There's been enough good ore to keep going, though, Gus," May responded.

"Still, this is the second tunnel. That's a lot of years down the drain."

"If we hit it big, they'll have been years well spent." May sat down in the dirt beside Al and leaned against a fallen log. Overhead, a sudden breeze swished through the pines. The air held the arid smell of autumn—a blend of dry grasses and parched soil. Serviceberry leaves were already gold, especially where the sunlight glimmered on them.

"There's a nice little streak of galena where you're digging, Gus," Al spoke up. "Who knows? The Hercules could strike the mother lode any day now."

"Or maybe it'll just be another dry old hole," Gus replied.

The three of them sat in companionable silence for a few minutes. Al rested his head against the log and dozed off.

It was backbreaking work inside the mountain. They'd all taken turns, even Dad Reeves, despite his age. They'd roped family and friends into helping, too. Swinging a pick until it connected with jarring rock. Prying heavy chunks off the ceiling and walls. And then mucking. Always, there was the mucking. Bending, scooping, and lifting the waste rock and dirt into the ore car and pushing it out of the mine. May was glad she wasn't built like a bird. Some of her weight these days was sheer muscle, and she needed every bit of it.

"I guess Ed didn't hear me holler. He never came to eat," Al said as he sat up.

"He said he wanted to finish that little pocket he was digging, and then he'd come. I'll send him out." Gus started toward the tunnel and then turned back to them. "Oh, Ed's sister was up here to see the mine the other day—she and another nice woman named Myrtle White."

"Think they're interested in investing?"

"No. Just looking." Gus's face turned red. "They brought a nice picnic for us."

"Hmmm . . . It sounds like they came to see the miners, not the mine," May blurted out.

"Well, maybe so," Gus mumbled, still blushing. The sparkle was back in his eyes. "It took them half the day to climb up here. That Miss White, she's from Colfax, way down in Washington. She's a beauty." Then with a little smile he ducked his head and turned away.

May turned to Al and her jaw dropped. He looked back at her, grinning. Everyone seemed to be pairing up these days. Harry Day's sister, Eleanor, and that handsome scrappy Irishman, Ed Boyce, who headed up the Western Federation of Miners, were the latest. And Harry himself seemed pretty serious about that rancher's daughter, Nellie Dwyer, whose family lived near the Cataldo Mission.

Maybe what Gus needed was a wife. She'd have to be an independent sort, and hardy enough to live in an out-of-the-way mining town. Colfax, though. Pretty Miss White might lure Gus away from the mine, and then where would the Hercules partners be? In a bad spot, that's where.

Al lighted a lantern and took May's hand as they entered the tunnel, stepping around a pile of empty tin cans. Gus had gone ahead, and May could hear voices. Ed must be on his way out. Al paused for a moment to let their eyes adjust.

May let go of his hand long enough to stuff her unruly hair under her canvas hat and hitch up her overalls. After that long climb up the mountain, she didn't feel much like mucking. But when did any of them want to muck? The key to getting rich was to jump in and work hard—to sweat their way through the drudgery until they got results, whether they felt like it or not.

She took Al's hand again and they began the long walk into the mountain, following the narrow gauge track to the end of the tunnel.

CHAPTER 35

February 1900

May stood in the Wallace post office, ripped off the parcel's brown wrapper, and ran her hands over the smooth cover of the book. Would you look at that? She, May Arkwright Hutton, was a published author. Here it was, a real book with her name and the title, *The Coeur d'Alenes; or, A Tale of the Modern Inquisition in Idaho,* printed boldly across the cover.

The printing and engraving company in Denver had done nice work. May opened the stiff maroon cover and scanned a few pages. She hoped her text wasn't slanderous, but she had things to say about certain mine owners who exploited workers. The photographs had reproduced nicely, too, though no credit had been given to Nellie Stockbridge and her employer, Nate Barnard.

Before the book went to press, several hundred copies had already sold among labor organizations across the mining region. She loved to think of her story being read by so many people. Now it would be distributed all over the Northwest, where it could become a force for labor.

May took a deep breath and straightened her hat. She tucked the book deep into her coat, where it would be safe from the driving snow as she walked home. It would sit permanently on the end table by the rocking chair, she decided, so she could show it to everyone who visited.

She hurried up the mountain lane, partly to get out of the storm and partly because she could hardly wait to show Al.

"Look at this, honey!" May called out as she burst through the cabin door.

Al was sitting by the stove, sharpening a hand drill from the mine.

"Your book!" He put the drill on the floor and stood up eagerly. "Let's see."

She brushed crumbs from the table before setting the book there. Al rinsed his hands in the basin of warm water on the stove and dried them on a flour-sack towel. They sat down together, May still in her wet coat. He carefully opened the cover and turned the pages one by one, stopping here and there to read a few words or look at one of the illustrations. He lingered over the pictures, especially the ones of the bull pen.

"I'm proud of you." Al leaned over and hugged her. Then he took her hand in his. "This calls for a celebration. How about a party here at the cabin? I'll invite everyone we know and make up a big spread."

Al knew her, all right. She loved gatherings. And whether or not it was proper and modest, she loved being the center of things, too.

"Heck, I'd love that." May finally took off her coat and went to hang it on the peg by the door. "I'd want Gus and Harry and Dad to come, of course. And Grace and Ed. The Boyces. I sure do wish Jim Wardner hadn't moved away. He's someone I'd like to see again."

"Me, too. Mining towns don't hang on to folks very long."

"Wallace has sure hung onto us, though. In a few months, it'll be thirteen years."

Al nodded, absently rubbing a scab on the back of his hand.

"Are you happy here, May?" He stood, walked over to her, and helped her unwind the wet woolen scarf around her neck. "Do you ever wish for a different life?"

"Damn right I wish for a different life! I want to be rich. But I wouldn't change anything else—especially being married to you."

"I wouldn't change that part either—not for the entire world." Al gave her shoulder a pat. "And maybe the book will bring in some money."

"I hope so. But I'm counting on the Hercules for that."

"What if it never does? We might never find anything up there."

"I don't want to give up, if that's what you mean."

"No, I don't want to give up either. I just mean if those little stripes of ore fizzle out. Or if Gus quits." Al hung the wet scarf behind the stove and then went to the window. It wasn't yet mid-afternoon, but already the light was fading.

"There's something subdued about Gus these days," May agreed. "We need to get him to town more often. He's stuck in that dark tunnel all the time."

"Let's invite the beautiful Miss Myrtle White up to Wallace. He sure perked up when he told us about her."

"She might lure him away to Colfax. And Dad's too old for all that work."

"Yep. Dad told me the other day he's a Civil War veteran. We were sharpening picks at the mine and he got to telling stories about it." Al turned to face her. He needed a haircut, but Dad had been too busy at the mine to do much barbering. "Let's finish planning this party. I've got another lodge meeting tonight, so I'll have to leave right after supper."

May got her pen and a piece of paper and lighted the lamp, noting that the globe was sooty again. Cleaning it was her least favorite chore, but the longer she ignored it, the dimmer the light grew. In this dark, wintry time of year they needed all the light they could get.

May shook her head and began writing the guest list, putting Gus's name at the top.

CHAPTER 36

February 1900

MAY SCOOPED THE LAST OF THE MORNING'S ASHES FROM THE STOVE and shut the metal door with a clang. She knew better than to clean the cabin for a party before she scraped the grate. No matter how careful she was, the fine ashes stirred themselves into a cloud of gray dust that floated into the room and settled on the furniture, rugs, and the hurricane lanterns.

Usually Al took care of cleaning the stove, but she had sent him to the store. She had no idea how many people would show up to congratulate her for her literary success, but the worst thing would be to run out of food. She waited a few minutes for the ashes to settle before grabbing her dust cloth. Al said she was to be a queen for the day. He would serve the coffee and May's three-egg cake so she could just enjoy the company. The guests—everyone from miners to shopkeepers, from union supporters to neighbors—would drift in throughout the afternoon, since the cabin could hold only so many at a time. May dragged another chair into the main room and straightened the rug.

As she polished the hurricanes, she pondered what to wear. Something fancy that would stand out—maybe her deep blue satin with the ruffled lace at the bodice, except it probably needed pressing. She hated ironing. The only thing that made it tolerable was to prop open a good book on the shelf beside the ironing board. Otherwise, pushing a hot iron over lengths of fabric was just plain tedious.

She worried that she may have offended some of Al's fellow Masons with her novel—and, worse than that, their sister members in the new Order of the Eastern Star, which May had just joined. If those women were put out by her book, things could get unpleasant.

Her thoughts were cut short by Al pushing through the door, his arms laden with canvas tote bags.

"I got more coffee," he said, setting the bags on the floor. "And some walnuts in the shell from Spokane. They weren't too expensive, so I bought enough to fill up your big bowl. Maybe people would like to crack their own. Oh, and I saw Jim Wardner in town. He lives out near the coast someplace now, but he's here for a couple of weeks looking into his business interests. I invited him. He'll be glad to see how you've come up in the world."

"Oh, I'd love to see him again. He gave me my first cooking job over in Eagle City, remember?" May wiped the red checkered oilcloth covering the table. "Here, honey. Let's set things out. People might start coming soon. I'd better put on my dress, too. I think I'll wear the gold one."

"I also saw Ed Boyce at the store." Al began unloading the bags. "People were clustered around him while he talked union business again. That fella is quite an organizer. The union wouldn't be nearly as powerful without him. Harry's sister, Eleanor, was there with him, so maybe the rumor that he's courting her is true. The two of them might stop by today."

"Good." May's voice was muffled as she pulled her skirts over her head in the bedroom. "It'll be nice to see everyone. This winter has stretched on too long." She twisted her hair into a loose chignon and fluffed her curly bangs.

"There's Gus now, climbing the lane." Al poured the walnuts into the bowl.

May glanced at herself in the mirror. Her cheeks were flushed pink with excitement. She was glad she didn't have those telltale creases around her eyes like other women her age. She was lucky that way; her extra weight filled out her face so she looked younger than her thirty-nine years. Her figure might be matronly, but at least her face was still smooth.

Al opened the door when he heard Gus stomping snow from his boots on the porch.

"C'mon in, Gus! Glad you're out of that tunnel today."

"I wouldn't miss a party for May now, would I? I came early to show you folks some ore samples."

"Hello, Gus. Spread those samples on the bed. Let's take a look." May uncovered her cake and set it on the table.

"Well, they're nothing much, but there's a little capillary I've been digging away at." Gus scooped some rocks out of his pockets and dropped them on the quilt. "Seems those capillaries never turn into anything important, though."

May picked up a sample, scrutinized it, and handed it to Al. "Feel how heavy it is. What do you think?"

"It sure looks good to me."

"Well," Gus said slowly. "That's what I thought, too. Doc and I'll follow it for a bit longer. If it doesn't turn into something bigger, I dunno ..."

"Maybe there's a whole mountainful of silver in there, Gus." May picked up another sample. "Don't you go getting dejected on us now."

Gus gave her a wink. "This isn't the time to talk about discouragement. We're celebrating today. I'm glad your book is published. I haven't read it, but I hear it tells quite a story."

"You bet it does, Gus. I didn't mince any words, either. I'll show you the photos in it. There are some people you'll recognize, believe me."

CHAPTER 37

Al Hutton – February 1900

He stepped outside the back door and stood quietly for a moment on the well-packed path to the woodpile. The fire in the stove needed another log or two, but there was no hurry. Maybe he'd just stay here for a minute to drink in the peace and quiet.

In the evening light, he gazed down at Wallace. Electric lights glittered from the downtown. Every day, the view seemed to change. Even in tonight's deep snow, there was a new building going up. The narrow river was bordered with ice, but he knew the dirty water was surging down the channel with a vengeance. He hoped it wouldn't flood the downtown again this spring. When the miners had stripped the hillsides of trees, they'd turned the stream into a roaring river looking to get even.

Behind him, the cabin buzzed with activity. May was in her element, bustling everywhere at once, making sure her guests were well fed and content. She looked beautiful in that fancy gold dress. The color was high in her cheeks, and her eyes sparkled. She seemed more energized with every new person who came. He was glad he'd planned this day for her. It was nice, though, to slip away for a minute. He enjoyed their friends, of course, but as the afternoon faded into evening, he felt himself fade along with it. Crowds of people exhausted him. Give him a quiet corner any day.

Lamplight shone from the window. People had been dropping in all afternoon and there were more to come. Right now, a little crowd was sitting near the stove, listening closely and hooting as May read aloud from her book. She was right: Her novel didn't mince words. He was proud of her, but he sure hoped she hadn't stepped on too many toes. With Wallace suffering from labor turmoil, May's story might be like pouring fuel on a fire.

She was more at ease around men, but plenty of women were here, too. There were even a couple of those red-light girls from town. They'd stood on the porch, nervous as schoolgirls, until May swept to the door and invited them in. She made them feel like princesses, making sure they had a comfortable place to sit before slicing wedges of cake for them. Somehow, she skillfully drew them into the conversation. He loved that about May. She always took care of the common folks.

Harry and Nellie were here, and Jim Wardner. Gus sat cracking walnuts at the table. Miss Stockbridge sat to the side, watching the others. The Dawsons had brought along their year-old baby. What a cute little thing she was, stuffing cake into her mouth and clutching that rag doll. He sure did wish he and May had children. Wouldn't it be something to have a little tyke to take to baseball games and bounce on his knee? He could picture a miniature May, climbing trees and reciting poems and chasing boys in the schoolyard. Children hit a soft spot in his heart. After all this time, though, it seemed certain that he and May weren't ever going to be parents.

Laughter burst from the cabin. May was standing now, gesturing grandly with her book in one hand. Her hair was falling from its place, as usual. It curled around her face in the lamplight. His chest lifted. Even after all these years, he could still barely believe his good fortune. How he, a plain and simple orphan, could have ended up with such an extraordinary woman was beyond him. May was like a fire inside him. He couldn't imagine life without her.

Standing here wasn't keeping the stove going, though. Besides, his boots were soaked through. He began loading his arms with firewood. The wind was picking up. Overhead, it swished through the trees with a soft sound that reminded him of steam escaping a boiler. He missed the old locomotive with its rumbling power, warm firebox, and distinctive whistle. It was good to be removed from the labor clashes, though. He still had bad dreams about that gun pressing into his ribs.

That poor devil, Paul Corcoran, got in a peck of trouble when the Bunker Hill and Sullivan building got blown to pieces. Someone had to take the blame for those two deaths. It had been hard to prove that Corcoran, who was union secretary at the time, might be guilty until one witness said he saw Corcoran riding atop a boxcar that fateful day. An impressive new attorney, William Borah, had clinched the case by reenacting the speeding boxcar ride. Corcoran got sentenced to hard labor.

Al continued loading his arms with firewood. His shoulder was complaining again. Carrying his usual heavy load was getting a bit harder now that he was almost forty. Not that he was old yet. Still, there were a few reminders that he wasn't as young as he used to be, like this ache that started after swinging a pick with Gus last week. He didn't know how Gus did it day after day.

May said Gus was getting discouraged. Well, he himself was a little disheartened, too, although he hadn't mentioned it to anybody, not even May. Some days he looked at the mountain and studied how enormous it was. What were the chances that Gus's tiny, twisting tunnels would hit the exact spot where the riches lay? No one even knew if there actually was good silver inside that vast expanse of rock and dirt. A few capillaries here and there didn't always promise a mother lode.

It didn't do any good to falter, though. Persistence was the only thing that ever paid off.

He forced his attention back to the woodpile. With his free arm, he covered the neatly stacked logs with the old piece of heavy canvas he used to keep the snow off. Then he turned and made his way along the icy path to the cabin, taking one last look in the window. May was bending over the Dawson child now, wiping cake from the baby's pink mouth. As he watched, she leaned in and kissed the little girl on the top of her head.

Al's throat tightened. May loved children as much as he did. She would have made a remarkable mother.

CHAPTER 38

July 1900

It seemed to May that spring had come and gone in the blink of an eye. The yellow flowers on the mountainside had dried to crisp husks in the hot sun, and the creek where she drew water was just a trickle. The afternoons were brick-oven hot. It was a different kind of heat than back home in Ohio, though. Idaho had none of the Midwest's suffocating humidity. By evening, when shadows stretched across the mountains and night hawks swooped overhead, the warmth was gone. Nights were so cool that she and Al often slept under the quilt.

She started down the lane to town, swinging her shopping bag and rehearsing what she'd say if she ran into any of the Masons or Eastern Star women. People sure did get offended easily. But the statements in her book were absolutely true. It was time for folks to hear things in plain English and not get huffy about it.

The book had started to bring in a small profit, which helped with the loss of Al's railroad wages. Now, every cent they didn't need to survive was going to buy supplies for the Hercules. She made her grocery money last weeks, with help from her garden. All summer, she coaxed vegetables from the mountain soil. The short season made it difficult, but last year she'd grown enough beans, pumpkins, potatoes, and beets to get through the winter.

The general store was empty. She stepped inside and stood for a few seconds, enjoying the smell of freshly ground coffee and the earthy fragrances wafting from bins of flour and legumes. She loved this place and the easy camaraderie she'd had for years with the storekeeper. May found the canned milk she needed and placed it on the counter.

"Hey, Elmer, you gonna make me wait all day?" She could hear him lugging crates in the back room. He poked his head out, a pipe clenched in his teeth, sweat glistening on his forehead.

"Sorry, Mrs. Hutton. I was making so much noise I didn't hear you come in."

"I could have robbed you! Just be glad I'm honest," May kidded him, tracing the decorative flourishes on the side of the brass cash register with her finger. "Have you read my book yet?"

"Uh, yes." The storekeeper took a nervous puff on his pipe. "That's quite a story you've got there."

"You like it?"

"Have you sold many copies?" He dodged her question.

"Yes, quite a few. People say it strikes a chord with them."

"Well, it sure does strike something. Will that be all for you today?" He wiped his forehead with his handkerchief and counted out May's change. "You'd best hurry on home now, Mrs. Hutton. It feels like a thunderstorm is coming."

A thunderstorm. What a phony excuse! The man just didn't want her in his store any longer than necessary. He was afraid she'd scare off his business. She picked up her bag.

"Elmer, I'll get out of your store now." She winked. "You wouldn't want me to scare away those nice folks who are killing our miners, would you?" She pulled the door shut hard behind her before he could answer.

That was the trouble with this town. No one was willing to stand up for a cause. It sure did hurt when someone you'd known for years hurried you out the door just because you tried to right a social wrong. She wished she could take her business elsewhere, but that meant a trip all the way to Wardner just to pick up a can or two for the pantry.

May turned toward the butcher shop and then changed her mind. Buying meat could wait until tomorrow. She was in no frame of mind to shop anymore. Right now, she'd go home and scrub the cabin from one end to the other. Then she'd make Al a nice bean soup for dinner, in case he got home from the Hercules in time.

She regained her composure thinking of Al. He always had that effect on her. Without even being here, he could soothe her and put everything into perspective. May knew she sometimes blew things out of proportion. So what if a small-town shopkeeper didn't like the things she said in her book?

She hoped Al would come home early. Recently he'd been staying up at the mine until dusk. Then he would hunch over the ledger books on the kitchen table, figuring assessments. He was discouraged about the way things were going up there, she could tell. He never said so, but some nights he seemed to be making an effort to sound optimistic. She was feeling it, too. It was tough to pour years of time and money into a venture that never paid off. There were days when she wondered if it was ridiculous to be tunneling into that gigantic mountain with tiny picks and shovels. She was determined not to quit, but staying hopeful year after year was hard.

They had to, though. She and Al and Gus were like the timbers that shored up the mine tunnel. Without them, the whole thing might come tumbling down.

She started up the mountain lane. Everything seemed gloomy. Even the sky had clouded over. It was indeed starting to look like a thunderstorm. Maybe she had read more into Elmer's comments than he had intended. Maybe he had been watching out for her after all.

CHAPTER 39

September 1900

MAY'S EYES SWEPT THE VALLEY AND SETTLED ON DOWNTOWN WALLACE. The door to the Flash in the Pan Saloon opened and a drunk stumbled into the street. So many of the miners were hard drinkers who squandered their wages on liquor and women. The number of saloons and red-light girls attested to that. If only they would wise up. May sighed and turned to her packing.

She and Al were heading up to the mine again this afternoon. By now she was used to hauling supplies on her back. Al took the heaviest loads, but she carried her share. This summer, she had made them each a sturdy canvas backpack to help distribute the weight. At the moment, they lay empty on the cabin floor, a tangle of cotton straps, buckles, and green pouches. It sure would be nice to have a couple of workhorses.

The two of them would spend the night and put in a full day's work tomorrow while the good weather held out. The tent was already up there, thank goodness, along with some old quilts airing on a makeshift clothesline. This time, she was taking a pillow for each of them, even if she had to tie them to the outside of her pack. The last few nights in the tent, she and Al had wadded up extra shirts and tried to cradle their heads on them. They'd awakened with stiff necks and a morning's worth of grumpiness. A person had to have a few comforts.

A dizzy spell took her by surprise and she sat down abruptly in the rocking chair. She'd had a few similar bouts in the past year, along with an unusual number of nosebleeds. At first, she had hoped she might be pregnant, but she wasn't. Al thought the altitude was starting to bother her. They'd lived in the mountains for thirteen years, though, and it had never been a problem before. Usually the dizziness didn't last long, nor did the nosebleeds. Hell, she didn't let it worry her. More annoying were the dull headaches she sometimes got. They set her teeth on edge.

She sat perfectly still, waiting for the dizziness to subside. Then she rose and began wrapping some dried beans. Once they reached the mine, she would soak and simmer them with salt pork for tomorrow's meals. By now, the crude little cabin at the entrance held a few pots and pans, some cracked dishes, and a rickety table covered with the old oilcloth from her diner. The battered stove in the corner was as finicky as an old mule but it was adequate.

There were footsteps on the porch, and Al came through the door.

"Almost ready?" he asked before he glanced at the still-empty packs on the floor. Then he added, "Need some help?"

"I'm more ready than it seems. The food just needs to be put in the packs. Do you want to take some gloves this time? Your hands are getting so beat up."

"Nope," Al answered. "My hands are fine. Nellie wanted Harry to wear gloves, too, so his hands would look nice for their wedding. It's easier to work without them, though. I don't mind a few scrapes and cuts."

"All right. Here, honey, could you put this squash in the bottom of your pack? Then the beans and the bread on top." May sat down again. "Do you mind carrying the extra candles, too?"

Al looked over at her. "Are you all right?"

"Just a little dizzy. I'll be fine. Let's load the flour and extra shirts in mine. Then I'll tie the pillows on the back."

"Pillows?"

"I know it will look ridiculous, but who cares? We'll appreciate them come nighttime. I bought some new socks for Gus, too. We can throw those in on top."

137

Al grinned as he good-naturedly cinched the pillows onto May's bulging pack. "You're going to look like a walking snowman."

When they reached the mine that afternoon, Gus was dumping a load of muck over the mountainside. Behind him, ninebark leaves—always the first to show fall colors—glowed red in the sun. Gus waved as they trudged through the trees and slid their packs to the ground.

"Did you bring me a pie, May?"

"No, sorry, Gus. Just some good old staples this time. We'll have a nice tender squash and bread with butter, though. And I'll make my famous baked beans for tomorrow. How's that?"

"Good. Sometimes these meals of yours are all that keep me going."

"Me, too," Al said. "What's new up here?"

"Nothing at all. I've been doing some thinking, though. Here's what I've decided: I'm going to spend one more year up here, and if we don't strike something big by then, I'm going to... well, I'm going to have to . . . uh . . ."

May stared at him. Al stuck his hands in his pockets and drew a deep breath.

May finally spoke. "Have to what?"

Gus bent and picked up a pebble. "To be honest, I'm not sure. I just know I've spent a lot of years digging for nothing. I need to make a better life."

"We sure do appreciate what you do up here," Al said mildly. "And we'd be in a whole lot of trouble without you."

"Well, I'd never leave you folks in the lurch," Gus answered. "I'm just thinking ahead, that's all."

CHAPTER 40

Al Hutton – May 1901

That underground water they blasted into last week sure had made a mess of things. It gushed into the tunnel, driving him and Gus out. When they were finally able to go back in, the tunnel was wet and slippery, and the moisture swallowed up their puny candlelight like a black, rainy night. Dampness clung to his clothes until his shirt felt as though he'd dunked it in the creek. Worse than that, his worn-out work boots had gaping holes in each toe, so his feet got cold and wet.

All that water made mucking a lot harder. The dirt was heavy mud now. By the end of the day, his shoulders and back ached as if he were a flabby desk clerk tunneling for the first time. In truth, he'd lugged hundreds of loads from the mine, until the piles spilling down the mountainside looked like enormous rock slides.

That little vein of ore, though!

They were following it feverishly, hoping it would widen into something big. Even Harry, who hated working underground, was up here all the time, pitching in. Doc surprised them all with his staying power, and Gus had animation back in his voice when he talked about it. Of course, it could be like all the other capillaries they'd found. After a few feet every one of them had petered out.

This one seemed to be holding its own. Yesterday it had narrowed disappointingly, but this morning it had broadened again, dark and glittery in contrast to the lighter rock surrounding it. Every miner knew that sometimes these little veins led to a bigger body of ore. The tunnel twisted and turned as they pursued the brownish-black streak.

He and Gus and Harry hadn't slept much. They just kept blasting away at the rock, stopping only to wolf down a big meal now and then. Their work clothes were caked with dried mud, and their faces were streaked with sweat and dirt.

May had practically worn herself out helping them muck. He couldn't believe how indomitable she was. Right now, she was busy inside the hut at the mouth of the tunnel making another batch of baked beans for them to eat while she went to town to get more provisions. He loved the fact that May wasn't afraid to make the trip alone. She didn't care a whit about having a proper escort and declared she'd know what to do if she met a moose—or a drunken miner with ill intentions—on the way. At least there was a primitive road that led up here now. It made the trip easier.

At the last minute, Harry decided to go to town with her. He stuffed his dirty pockets with choice pieces of ore to take to the assay office. He wanted to send a note to his ma and pa, too, he said. They were intensely interested in their son's venture. Harry often sought their advice.

"You'll have to keep them mum, Harry," Gus told him as he left. "If this turns into something, we'll need time. We don't want to be overrun by outsiders trying to horn in."

"Ma and Pa won't say a word. They know better," Harry assured them as he fingered a piece of ore in his palm. "And I'll swear the assayer to secrecy, too. He's pretty good about keeping his mouth shut. But I think it's a good idea to find out the value of these samples."

"I agree." Gus picked up his tools again. "When you come back, bring those brothers of yours to help. It shouldn't be much longer before we know what we have here."

CHAPTER 41

June 1901

May poured hot water from the kettle into the washtub. It felt good to be home again. Camping out at the mine was all right, but a woman liked a few niceties in her life now and then—like a real privy and some clean clothes. She could hardly wait to wash her hair. Even her scalp felt gritty.

She spent the morning bathing and scrubbing the dirt from her overalls. Then she stood outside in the sunshine, letting the June breeze dry her hair. No matter how much she brushed it, her hair wouldn't lie smooth. It was still tangled and frizzy. She lost patience, wound it up quickly, and stabbed in some hairpins to secure it to the nape of her neck.

Wearing a dress felt cumbersome after spending the past few days in her mining overalls. Long skirts always got in the way. She was forever hitching hers up to see where she was going or to climb through the woods. Overalls were a distinct improvement. With a sigh, she grabbed her shopping bags and made her way downtown. The wild roses were blooming, filling the mountain air with their delicate scent.

It was mid-afternoon by the time she had finished buying provisions and lugging them back to the cabin. She was on good terms with Elmer at the store again. Leaving the sacks on the floor, she spread a length of new fabric over the tabletop. Gus wouldn't remove his ragged shirt long enough for her to mend the hole in the elbow, so she would make him a new one instead. Good thing flannel was economical. Al wouldn't mind that she had spent the money. She smoothed its soft gray surface with her hand. If she hurried, she could hand-stitch a simple work shirt by tomorrow night and take it up to the mine the following day. It was the buttonholes that slowed her down, although she was pretty fast at those tiny stitches by now.

Al opened the door and stepped inside, holding a broken dynamite detonator.

May rose to give him a hug. "I wasn't expecting you."

"I didn't think I'd be home today, but I have to take care of this detonator. Gus has been using it to set off charges, and he broke it this morning. It's slowing him down to be without it. We didn't have the right tools to fix it up there." Al glanced down at it doubtfully. "If I can't repair it, I'll have to buy another one so I can go straight back. Gus is working alone up there."

"Is the vein holding out?"

"It widened a little early this morning."

"That's good news if I ever heard it."

They spent the afternoon in companionable silence, May cutting and stitching Gus's shirt, and Al sitting on the floor fiddling with the detonator. Once in a while, May stopped her sewing to look over at him. She loved to watch Al work. He knelt on the worn plank floor and bent over his project, completely absorbed. His hands were fine-boned and meticulous despite the months of hard labor. Once in a while, he lifted his head and stared unseeing into the room, thinking about the best way to proceed. May was quiet, letting him concentrate. Thunder rumbled in the distance. She turned the flannel collar and stitched it in place.

All of a sudden, someone leaped onto the porch and began pounding on the door. Al startled and scrambled to his feet. May jumped up, darted to the door, and flung it open. There stood Gus, hair wild, eyes afire, with two red spots burning on his cheeks. He burst into the room, lugging his small battered suitcase, and heaved it onto the table. May's scraps of flannel went flying.

"Look at this!" Gus threw open the suitcase. It was full of rock samples that glittered in the lamplight. "Just look at this rock!"

Her heart still pounding, May gasped as she stared into the suitcase. She reached in and took out a heavy piece of ore. Al grabbed one, too. They inspected the gleaming pieces in their hands as Gus went on.

"I was digging up there after you left this morning, Al." Gus paused to catch his breath. "All of a sudden, I swung my pick and buried it up to the shaft. When I pulled it out, this ore came pouring down around me. I knew right then. This is it! The mother lode!"

May clutched the edge of the table for support. "Gus, old sport, you did it!"

"Whoa now, you two! It could just be another little pocket," Al said cautiously. But his hands were trembling.

"It's not. I dug some more, and the vein spread out in all directions. It's big." Gus shook his head, a slow grin spreading over his face. "I couldn't believe my eyes, so I lighted all the extra candles to be sure."

"All that work!" May impulsively reached out and gave Gus a hug. "It's going to pay off!" A hairpin came loose and her frizzy curls cascaded around her shoulders. She didn't bother to fix it.

Al seized another sample from the valise, but then paused, his hand still in midair.

"Gus, how do you know? It looks good, but are you sure it's rich ore?"

"I stopped by Harry's place, and we took it to the assay office. Swore them to secrecy. They took their time. Finally they told us it looks like the richest lead-silver ore they've seen around these parts. We'll have to wait for the formal assay, of course, but they liked their first look."

"Incredible!" Al rummaged eagerly through the dusty suitcase and then clapped Gus on the back. "I can't believe it!"

"Neither could I, but it's true."

At last! After all these years! May felt a fluttering in her chest as excitement bubbled up inside her. She could almost feel her wagon hitching itself to a star. And this was no ordinary star. She put her hand over her heart. There was no telling what would happen, but the possibilities took her breath away.

CHAPTER 42

June 1901

After Gus left, Al took May's hand and pulled her close. She could feel his heart beating fast. "Can you believe it, May? This is the day we've been waiting for!"

"Oh, honey, just think!" May brushed away the hair that had fallen over his forehead. Her mind was careening in a hundred directions at once. "I can't even fathom it all."

"We shouldn't get our hopes up until we get the assayer's official report. And until we're sure the vein widens more. I'm already getting all kinds of ideas, though."

"Me, too. Lots of them."

"I need to go up there right now to guard the entrance in case word leaks out."

She gave him a peck on the cheek. "I know. You be careful. I can just picture what might happen if people find out about this. Let me pack some things for you."

"I'll just take some bread and another shirt."

May watched him stride down the lane as her mind continued to spin. Good thing Harry was first rate at business affairs. He'd guide them in the right direction. He was in full agreement that they should never sell out to big business. The hard part would be keeping the discovery quiet and not letting on. There might be vultures waiting to swoop in.

This felt like a fairy tale. With a few—or a lot!—of pennies in her pocket, she and Al could live in style. Right away, she'd buy Al some boots and a suit of clothes; he hadn't had a new coat in ten years. She'd get some fine-looking dresses for herself, too, with hats to match and as much lace as she wanted. When the two of them were comfortable, she would use some of their newfound money to fund her projects. Suffrage. Lending a hand to exploited workers. Looking after poverty-stricken children. She could think of a hundred worthy places to distribute the wealth.

—◆—

Two days later, Al came home with the results of the ore analysis. The samples were thirty-eight percent silver, an astoundingly high percentage. May studied the official certificate and then let out a whoop. She did a silly little dance right there on the porch, with Al grinning all the while. "We're rich, honey! I'll bet some of the tailings we've been dumping over the mountainside are more valuable than what the Frisco and the Tiger are shipping to the smelter."

"You've got a point there. We'll have to check our waste piles, all right. Right now I need to hire a guy who can dynamite. Gus and Harry asked me to find someone. But listen, May, I've got an idea."

"What's that?"

"I know it's too soon, but there's a nice house for sale down on Pine Street. It's got two stories, a pretty front stoop, and plenty of windows. From what I can tell, there's a parlor in front and a dining room and kitchen toward the back. Three or four bedrooms upstairs."

"Oh, Al!" May drew in an eager breath.

"We'd have to wait until the money starts to come it. But it wouldn't hurt to take a closer look. Find out the price. I could see you in a place like that, May."

"Let's walk down there right now, could we? You can show me which one it is." She began untying her apron strings.

"Well, all right, if we hurry. I've got to find a dynamiter and get back up to the mine. Maybe I'll take Harry's brother Jerome with me to guard the tunnel. Get your hat and let's go."

She put on her best sun hat in celebration, the copper-colored one with the wide satin ribbons down the back. They fluttered in the breeze as if there weren't a care in the world as she and Al started down the lane.

After all these years, she still loved walking through town on Al's arm. Excitement quickened her steps. After a couple of blocks, Al turned onto Pine Street and stopped in front of a tall gray house nestled between two others. "This is it."

May's breath caught in her throat. She could certainly picture herself living here! The ground floor alone was two or three times as large as the cabin, and the second story looked even more spacious, since it jutted out over the front stoop. Across the front, three full-size windows glistened in the sunshine, framed inside by graceful curtains. Swirls of carved white trim adorned the eaves, serving no purpose except to look pretty. A little path of flat fieldstones led across the front yard to the door.

"Oh, honey!"

"I think the price might be affordable, now that we'll have more than two cents to our names. I can just see it, May. You could have guests to your heart's content, with room to spare. See how there's one bedroom in front there, and maybe a couple more in the back?"

"And a dining room. Wouldn't it be something to have a real dining room? We'd have to get some furniture." Elation bubbled up in May's voice. "A nice big table and matching chairs, for a start. And a couple of velvet parlor seats. Oh, and maybe a set of china and a china cabinet."

"No more hauling buckets from the creek, either. I'm sure there's running water."

"Let's get that ore out of the mountain so we can move in." May winked.

CHAPTER 43

Summer 1902

MAY SANK INTO THE COMFORTABLE PARLOR CHAIR AND TOOK A SATISFIED look around her new front room. Sunshine streamed through the windows onto the carpeting, lighting up its rich reds and blues. She loved how it set off the flowered wallpaper and ornate ceiling. This house made her shake her head in disbelief sometimes. Why, the kitchen alone was enough to make a woman think she was in heaven. The furniture was still sparse, but that would change.

Even the yard was gratifying. Its grassy lawn covered every bit of mud. White picket fences marched the length of the lot on both sides, flanked with pretty little gardens. She loved tending those rosebushes from Spokane. Having flowers made her feel like upper crust. She hoisted herself from the chair and went out the front door, buffing the brass knob as she went. Maybe that pink rosebud was ready for cutting.

"Hello, ma'am."

The little girl's voice came from behind the picket fence.

"Good morning! Where did you come from?"

"I'm staying here with Auntie Alice now. My mama and pa got drowned in a flood." A round, pale face peeked over the fence, framed by dark brown ringlets.

"Oh, sweetie, I'm so sorry!"

"I came on the train last night."

"What's your name?"

"Josie."

"Well, Josie, my name is May. I can tell we're going to be good friends."

"How come you're wearing pants and not a dress?"

"I like pants when I work in the yard."

"Oh. I never saw a lady wearing pants before."

"Well, Josie, you've seen one now. I'll tell you what. Run and ask Aunt Alice if you can come over for a cookie. Maybe you'd like to try on my fancy hats."

"All right!"

May bent and pulled a weed from the dirt. An orphan, right next door. Her neighbor could probably use some help with that. It wouldn't be easy to become a mother to someone else's child overnight. And May knew exactly what little girls needed: plenty of love, a warm lap for reading stories, cookies made just for you, and someone to teach you how to dress and fix your hair. Lord knows, she could have used some pointers in that direction herself. She'd desperately missed having a mother. Poor old Granddad had been at a loss when it came to a girl's frocks and hair ribbons. She'd had to figure those out for herself.

It was nearly dinnertime when Josie finished trying on hats and sampling May's gingersnaps.

"Would you like to come over again sometime?" May asked. "I was thinking about sewing a rag doll, and I need someone to tell me how the face should look."

"All right! I'll ask Auntie. Oh, and she says I have to call you Mrs. Hutton, not May."

"Well, all right. I suppose that's good manners. In that case, I'll call you Miss Josie. How does that sound?"

The little girl giggled. May put some cookies on a plate for her to take home and saw her to the door. Then she watched until Josie was safely next door. She'd have to tell Al about her. He would want to make a stick horse or something.

———

The next day, when Al came home from the Hercules, he looked grim. May took one glance at the straight set of his mouth and asked, "What's wrong?"

"Just about everything, that's what. We're in a bind up at the mine."

"Did someone get hurt?"

"No, thank goodness. Not that. But the railroad is refusing to haul the ore, and the smelter is refusing to take it."

"Why on earth?"

"Big business wants to buy us out. You know that huge trust company? They think the Hercules is worth millions and they're trying to force us to sell. Harry got a measly offer this morning."

"So they've got the railroad and the smelter in their back pocket." May's eyes snapped. "Those scoundrels. They'd better not trifle with us!"

"They're used to getting their way."

"What does Harry say?"

"He's madder than I've ever seen him. Even if they make a better offer, he'll never agree to sell. That whole mountain might be pure silver. But I'm worried. It could mean no income for us until we can work this out. That might take months or even years."

"Oh, Al, the house!"

"That's what I mean. We need our dividends." He sat down at the old kitchen table, his back rigid.

May sat beside him at a loss for words. The thought of the two of them giving up their new home while the mine shaft was backed up with loads of rich lead-silver ore made her want to scream. She could feel her cheeks getting hot.

"We'll sue the devils," she fumed.

"That's what Harry said, but with what? It takes money. We'd be brand-new underdogs fighting a huge trust. They've got their lawyers, their capital, their fingers in every pie except ours. How could we expect to win?"

Those crooks! Trying to force a sale by whatever shady means possible! It was wrong, plain and simple. There must be plenty of ways to fight back. Harry had probably already thought of a few. She'd come up with some of her own. Writing irate letters to the governor had worked when Al was locked up in the bull pen.

"This could be a disaster, May. I hate to even think about it."

May got up and brought Al a cup of coffee, sweetened just the way he liked it. Then she sat down again, took his hand in hers, and gently rubbed it. It was so unfair. Just when the two of them were finally going places!

One of her dizzy spells was coming on, but she wanted to raise hell. Those troublemakers would get the Hercules over her dead body.

CHAPTER 44

Summer 1902

Dear Lyman,

You would never believe the changes here this past year. The Hercules is producing the richest lead–silver ore ever found in these parts. Finally, our persistence is paying off!

Unfortunately, we think the railroads and smelters are in collusion with a huge trust corporation that's trying to force us out. The railroads have been an enormous impediment (they don't want to transport our ore), and some of the smelters have declined to take us, since we've REFUSED TO SELL OUT. That gigantic corporation meddles in everything. Between Al, me, our friend Harry Day, and a few others, we've been able to find our ways around them, though. Al is in Tacoma right now, visiting a smelter there that looks promising. Harry says we may need to buy our own. In the meantime, legal wheels are turning slowly. We've gone out on a limb to take on the trust company and are hoping we'll win. Idaho's leading attorney, William Borah, is representing us.

Despite all the difficulties, we've been able to expand the mine and are getting generous dividends *for now. The old trail up the mountainside is now a well-used, serviceable road. We've hired a crew and purchased new machinery. And ever since the* Spokesman Review got wind of our success, we've had a steady stream of curiosity-seekers making their way to the mine for a look.

I spend my time in town (no more lugging food and supplies up the mountain!), where we've purchased a charming two-story house. We have a large dining room, all fitted out for big parties. When I serve up a spread on our long table, it looks like a feast for a king—or maybe I should say a queen! So far, I've entertained Al's lodge here, the graduating class from the high school (which is right next door to us), and my new literary group—the Shakespeare Club.

The Episcopal Church is right around the corner. Al and I attend, although not regularly. We like listening to our friend Bishop Ethelbert Talbot when he's here to give the sermon. The neighborhood is growing quickly. New houses are going up, and everybody is planting maple and birch and alder trees. Our old friend and partner, Gus Paulsen, bought a stately house a couple of blocks from us. He has a fiancée, Miss Myrtle White, who will become his bride in September. Myrtle is quite a sport. Even though she's from Colfax—a whole day's trip from here—we got acquainted with her the minute we realized Gus was serious. He keeps pretty quiet about his personal affairs, but we were tipped off when he shaved his beard and then had some beautiful silver buttons made for her from the first of the Hercules ore.

I'm enclosing a couple of photographs so you can see what our life here in Wallace is like. Our local photographer, Nellie Stockbridge, and her boss, Nate Barnard, toted their heavy camera equipment to the mine shortly after Gus made the big discovery. The first picture I'm sending shows the glory hole itself. It doesn't look like much when I study it now, but that jagged hole in the mountain is our mother lode! The other photograph shows a group of us in the old shack at the mouth of the tunnel, examining chunks of ore by candlelight. You can see me there on the left.

Speaking of photographs, I have an old image of Granddad, tiny and faded, and decided to commission a large portrait to be made of it. It turned out well, so I've hung it in our dining room as a remembrance.

I've got all kinds of plans now that I am a "lady of leisure." I've been thinking about running for office, maybe the Idaho state legislature.

They could use an outspoken Democrat to represent the miners. I also want to expand my suffrage work. You can bet I exercise my right to vote in every election here in Idaho, but I fret about women in other states—especially Washington—who don't have that freedom.

Al is busy with his lodge and he's begun to look into investing. Both of us would like to travel. I hope to come east to visit you and the rest of the family, and I'd love to take a trip to Mexico. With our newfound wealth, traveling seems possible.

I'm not bragging about my wealth, Lyman. But those of you who thought I should never come west were wrong, pure and simple. If I'd heeded your advice, I'd still be poor old May, slaving over a hot stove in Ohio for pennies a day. Out here, I've found Al, my fortune, and all the social causes a woman could want. There's even a lovely child next door who gives me an opportunity to mother a little girl on occasion. Since Al and I don't have children of our own, we've learned to "borrow" them from others. Little Josie fills my spare time with make-believe tea parties, storybooks, and bug collecting.

Al and I also enjoy going camping and fishing these days. We pick a sunny day, pack up our tent, and go somewhere nice. Our favorite place is the Shadowy St. Joe River—a beautiful stream not far from here that lives up to its name. I even wrote a poem about it. Someday we'd like to build a summerhouse there.

I've begun rounding up and buying back all the copies of my book that are floating around. It's gotten a bit uncomfortable being the author of a story that denigrates mine owners, now that I am one myself. I also worry about lawsuits; I've become more aware of such possibilities since we now have assets to protect. So…please toss that copy I sent you into the fire.

Until I can schedule a trip to see you, how would you like to come to Wallace? It would be quite an adventure for you to see part of the Wild West. I'd happily buy you a train ticket and make sure you were nice and comfy in one of our new guest bedrooms. Think about it, won't you?

I guess that's all for now.

Love, May

CHAPTER 45

Al Hutton – Spring 1903

He stopped the push mower in the mid-morning shade and sat on the front steps to rest, looking critically at the lawn. May was bustling about inside the house, setting the dining-room table with her best dishes and silverware.

It was hard to believe. Ella Wheeler Wilcox, the famous poet, was coming to Wallace, and he and May were having her to supper. May had a way of arranging these things. Mrs. Wilcox wasn't the first well-known person to visit the Hutton home. Their attorney, William Borah, had taken a meal with them not long ago, among others. May had acquaintances in all kinds of lofty places. She was even talking about inviting Teddy Roosevelt when he was here on a whistle-stop visit.

He fetched the clippers and began to trim along the fence line, breathing in the smell of freshly cut grass. He and May had spent part of the morning extending the table so it stretched from the dining room all the way into the front room. It would seat twenty-five guests. Yesterday she'd polished her goblets and silverware. He knew from experience that now she would bake her pies and then start the main dishes. At the last minute, she'd toss away her stained apron, put on a frilly dress, and greet her company as though entertaining were absolutely no trouble at all.

Imagine the two of them hosting someone as prominent as Mrs. Wilcox! Most of that was due to May and the direct path she made toward her goals. But the Hercules got part of the credit. Thankfully, they'd found a way around the trust corporation's attempts to force them out. The independent smelter they were using was helping bring in plenty of dividends. The legal issue wasn't settled yet, not by a long shot, but with William Borah in charge, the outlook wasn't so grim.

He moved to the side yard and began trimming along the fence that divided their property from the neighbor's. Little Josie wasn't outside today, as she usually was. It sure was refreshing to have a child around. He loved the way she galloped everywhere on that stick horse he'd made for her and made him chuckle with her funny questions.

Lately he'd been wondering if moving to Spokane might be a good idea, although he hated to think about leaving their neighbors and friends. He and May—and Gus, too—had been talking about it. A bigger city held more opportunity for investing. Wallace was hemmed in by the mountains; there wasn't much space to expand. Downtown Spokane had plenty of room for the new buildings he and Gus were thinking about constructing.

It wouldn't hurt for May to be closer to a well-trained doctor these days, either. Her health just wasn't as vigorous as it used to be. There was nothing they could put a finger on, but some days she simply didn't feel good. Not that she let anything slow her down much. He noticed her sitting in the rocker more often, though, knitting or scribbling letters on her lap desk.

May wasn't sure she wanted to move to Spokane. She was well known in these parts. Running for the state legislature was next on her agenda. Also, after the hard-won victory for suffrage here in Idaho, May was reluctant to leave behind her right to vote. Maybe they'd best stay a couple more years.

He stood and surveyed his work. The yard looked tidy now. The walkway still needed some attention, but he'd get to that later. He glanced at his pocket watch. It was time to head uptown. There was a lodge meeting in half an hour and he needed to change his clothes. He put the clippers away and went in the back door. The house smelled wonderful, like freshly baked cinnamon-apple pie and May's golden flaky crust. Too bad he had to wait until supper to sample it.

Part III

Four Years Later

1907–1915

CHAPTER 46

Autumn 1907

MAY PUSHED ASIDE THE MAROON SATIN DRAPES AND STARED AT THE busy Spokane street below. Even at this early hour, wagons and automobiles crowded the intersection. Diagonally across from her, the steel framework for Gus and Myrtle Paulsen's eleven-story office building jutted into the sky.

The Hutton building in which she stood was a new four-story structure in the heart of Spokane's growing downtown. Its top floor was a spacious nine-room apartment where she and Al had just settled their feathers. They both missed the quiet Pine Street house in Wallace, but Al was correct: Spokane was the place for them. They needed a wider field for their projects. Al had already begun working on real estate investments. And although she hated to admit it, she needed to be near her competent big-city doctor. Something just wasn't right.

This handsome apartment had so much space that she hardly knew what to do with it. The living room was the size of a small ballroom, with hardwood floors, a heavy-beamed ceiling, and an ornately carved mantel over the fireplace. Tall windows overlooked the city. It was the perfect place for entertaining and holding committee meetings. May was spending a considerable amount of time buying furniture and decorating.

Some of their Wallace friends were already Spokane residents, and others were planning to move here soon. Gus and Myrtle and their children would occupy the top floor of the Paulsen Building when it was finished. They'd be a stone's throw away, although visiting would mean navigating long flights of stairs and a noisy intersection instead of a peaceful walk around the block.

She sure did regret having to leave behind the folks in Wallace, though, especially little Josie. Just thinking about her made May yearn to go back for another visit. Josie was a young schoolgirl now. May had taught her how to braid her own hair and darn her stockings and sew a simple apron. The girl could already make May's special pie crust, too. Together, they had written little poems and stories and sketched each other's portraits. Josie's big eyes had filled with tears when May told her she and Al were moving to Spokane.

May missed Harry and his family, too. And Dad Reeves. And Nellie Stockbridge. Nellie had never been a close friend, but she and May had a warm understanding about the value of women and their right to a fulfilling career. May doubted that Nellie would ever follow the migration to Spokane, despite the bigger opportunities here. The photographer was deeply attached to Wallace. She had an archive of pictures that thoroughly recorded the town's history.

May glanced at her calendar. Maybe next week she and Al could take the train to Wallace to see everyone. While Al visited his old lodge friends, she'd stop in at the miners' cafe to catch up with the boys. Then she'd head for Pine Street to find Josie.

Some folks had been angry when May and Al announced they were moving away. The serving girl at the lunch counter had accused them of "grabbing Idaho's riches and running off to Spokane," as if the Huttons were thieves deserting their hometown. Al, when he recovered from his shock at the girl's unblinking honesty, said he could see her point.

May knew that they would never forget the folks back home in Idaho. There were too many to name, but they all had a place in her heart. Al's, too. Just because the two of them moved to Spokane didn't mean they would abandon their old friends. Finally, they were in a position to help them.

Another thing she missed was the easy camaraderie she knew in Wallace: the familiar street corner exchanges, the front-porch visits, and the jovial banter with friends. She was new to Spokane and now she was rich—and, she admitted, overweight and flashy and prone to bluntly speaking her mind. It was the same story all over again: plenty of people avoided her, especially the well-heeled crowd. In Wallace, she had earned a grudging respect from even the most hoity-toity among them; here in Spokane she still needed to prove herself.

Not that there would be much time for leisurely visits here. By now, she had rolled up her sleeves and gotten to work. Someday she wanted to run for office again; her narrow defeat in Idaho in 1904 had encouraged her. Big business had backed her opponent, of course, but May had nearly won anyway. Heck, she had been disappointed, not discouraged. When time allowed, she would run for the U.S. Senate from Washington State.

For now, though, she had found a whole bushel-basket of projects calling for her attention. Most important was suffrage. Now that she had left Idaho, she felt like a second-class citizen again. She would help see to it that Washington women got the vote—and soon. She had big plans to stump the state with other suffragettes.

Then there was the Florence Crittenton Home for unwed mothers. Its residents—popularly known as "bad" girls, but really just healthy young women from dance halls or cheap hotels who had gotten carried away with a man, or were taken advantage of—often gave up their babies in disgrace, creating more orphans. As May saw it, each of them simply needed a good lonely man to marry her and turn a social stigma into a ready-made family. What a perfect solution for everyone—most of all, the innocent children. She'd have to look into the possibilities.

She was interested in the city's Charities Commission, too. And the need for a female police matron at the women's jail really got her blood flowing. There was work galore here in Spokane.

"Al, do you need the car this morning?" May asked as he sipped his coffee and read the *Spokesman Review* in the dining room. The high-ceilinged room was warm, even on a cold, rainy day like this one. "I have an interview with that newspaper reporter about the suffrage campaign."

"Go right ahead. I thought I'd work with the new office tenants downstairs. I'll call the driver for you. What time should I tell him?"

"Oh, I nearly forgot. He'll need the car to get it ready for tomorrow, won't he?"

Al's eyes sparkled at the thought of tomorrow's automobile race and their bright red Thomas Flyer. "He'll have time later on for that. Besides, there's not much more he can do. I'm hoping he'll just drive like a demon and win the trophy. The Flyer has the power to win, especially since the course is uphill. Some of those other cars are fine on the flats, but they can't handle the steep grade."

"I want to be there at the end and watch you two come steaming across the finish line." May stood behind him and rubbed his shoulders. "That would be almost as good as driving in last summer's Rose Carnival parade. Weren't we a hit down there in Portland—the car all covered with fresh roses and Abigail Scott Duniway in the backseat campaigning for suffrage?" She glanced fondly at her trophy on the windowsill. "Say, I thought you had a lodge meeting today."

"I do, but not until later. You go ahead to your interview and I'll reserve the car for this afternoon. Ten o'clock?"

"Yes."

May dressed carefully. No more homemade clothes for her! She had found a good dressmaker. But her outfits always needed fancying up. She managed that with her collection of hats, which were decorated with long plumes and cascades of brightly colored feathers. A zebra-striped coat had caught her attention the other day, and she was pondering buying it. Wouldn't it look grand on her, especially inside the red Flyer! She didn't care a whit what any of these Spokane people thought. That coat would make her stand out.

In her mind, she planned what to say to the reporter. She and her fellow Washington suffragists would work toward a vote in 1910, allowing plenty of time to wage an effective campaign. She would point out that suffrage was overdue here, and that women were intellectually suited to making good voting decisions. Besides, women were taxed on their holdings, and taxation without representation was a travesty. Oh, she could sure get fired up about suffrage.

Sometimes Al cautioned her, with a gentle smile and a wink, not to "make an unholy show" of herself as she worked. She knew he was right; she needed to temper her mining-camp language for these city folks. But, hell, she was comfortable being herself. That included saying what she thought, uncensored and in plain English.

If her energy flagged, she could revitalize herself with a nice leisure trip to a health resort. How she loved to travel! Not long ago, she had visited another of her favorite lawyers, Clarence Darrow, and his family in Chicago. Then she'd gone on to Ohio and Iowa to meet a few of Al's relatives and spend time with her half-siblings. How good it had felt to breeze back into her old hometown dressed in her finery, with $2,000 in her purse! She had shown them what their homely, loudmouthed half-sister had become, that was for sure.

CHAPTER 47

May 25, 1908

Dear Josie,

You won't believe what I saw this morning: a couple of daring squirrels chasing each other across a telephone line high above the busy street. I was afraid they would slip and fall, but they made it across the entire boulevard, even though the wire was swinging wildly from their weight. If they had tumbled off, they would have landed right on the fancy hat of Mrs. Fairweather, who was crossing the street at that moment.

I'm writing to see if you and your auntie can come visit for a few days. How does June 14 sound? I'll send train tickets, and of course you must stay here with Mr. Hutton and me. This apartment is big enough to hold an army of girls like you. You'll be our only guests, so I'll make sure you get the pretty room that overlooks the main intersection; it's fun to put crumbs on the window ledges there and watch the pigeons swoop in and gobble them up. Auntie Alice will be right across the hall.

Your room is furnished with a bed that has a royal-blue canopy, a comfy rocking chair for reading, and a soft rug on the floor. There's a pretty doll sitting on the coverlet. I bought her especially for you, so you can take her home when you go. Now that you're older, you'll understand that she's made of bisque, so she'll break if you drop her. She has brown hair (I think it might be real) and a lacy white dress with a matching hat. You'll love her tiny fingers and toes.

Also, I know you're almost too old for paper dolls, but maybe you can humor me and help me cut some from the Sears catalog. I sure do miss our cozy times spent snipping out their clothes at my kitchen table back in Wallace.

While you're here, we'll go for a ride along the river in our cherry-red car, stopping to dip our feet in the water. Then we'll climb to the top of the highest downtown building so you and Aunt Alice can see the view. I know you'll also want to bake a pie in my fancy new kitchen, just like old times. You're probably an old hand at it by now. And of course we'll have to take a look at the Spokane Falls you've heard so much about. It's thrilling to walk across the high metal bridge with the water roaring beneath you.

Most of all, of course, I'll want to hear about what's new with you, especially school. How's that boy who liked to pull your braids? Have you given him a piece of your mind yet?

Please show this letter to Auntie and ask her if you both can come. Then write back and let me know. Mr. Hutton will meet you at the station and bring you home to me—and I'll have your favorite gingersnaps waiting!

Love, May

CHAPTER 48

Winter 1909

MAY PULLED HER BLACK AND MAROON SCRAPBOOK FROM ITS GLEAMING shelf in the sitting room and ran her hand over the tattered cover. She could have bought a new blank book, but her habit of thrift died hard. It wasn't right to waste this perfectly good leather-bound ledger just because its pages were filled with old financial records. Her clippings could go right over the top of the neat columns of handwritten figures.

Among the clippings, she'd scattered letters, poems she had written herself, copies of her speeches, and whatever else seemed important, like Josie's little note, scrawled in girlish handwriting, thanking May for a "most spectacular" visit to Spokane. What fun they'd had! She had promised Josie there would be many more such occasions.

These scrapbooks gave a nice summary of the past several years. The Hutton name—both hers and Al's, in a quieter way—was always in the newspaper for one reason or another.

May took the scrapbook to the rocking chair. The chair's rich mahogany set off the multihued Oriental rug she'd ordered from Chicago. Her Tiffany lamps were lighted, warming the gray winter light that filtered in the windows. She was getting a late start today. Here she was, still in her lacy dressing gown, with her hair a tousled mess, but she just wasn't feeling well. Besides, she needed to find her copy of the speech she'd written for the Ladies Aid Society so she could use parts of it in her talk this afternoon.

At this point, though, she was pretty darned good at speaking off the cuff. She'd given so many pro-suffrage speeches in the past year it was second nature now. Sometimes she addressed seven or eight organizations a day. Then she would come home, take off her shoes, and spend time with Al while resting up for the next day, when the whirlwind would start all over again. Lately it had been exhausting. Al kept telling her to take it easy, and Lyman's latest letter had admonished her to slow down. But she had things to do.

The suffrage campaign was sure heating up. She was vice president of the Washington Equal Suffrage Association, but she was at odds with some of her fellow suffragists. Emma Smith DeVoe, the association's president, thought May's exuberant manner and full-steam-ahead tactics were damaging the cause. Mrs. DeVoe wanted a refined, tactful approach. But May knew a thing or two about taking command of a gathering and driving her point home. Everyone sat up and paid attention when she took the podium or led a parade, and her colorful speeches had picked up a lot of votes for suffrage. Heck, if DeVoe and her followers didn't like her strategies, it was just too bad. May represented all women, especially the common working girl. She intended to make sure that the everyday laundress, stenographer, and unwed mother had the vote, right alongside better educated, more cultured women. And when Washington women gained equality, May would move on to help other states.

This week, though, she wanted to take time to organize a fundraiser for Spokane's Home for the Friendless. The Democratic Party needed her attention, too. She had met and befriended her favorite candidate for president, William Jennings Bryan, who invited May to the Democratic National Convention. How could she miss a chance like that? Plus, she was planning a nice trip to Yellowstone Park with Al, if he could get away from his work with the building tenants and his new bank trusteeship.

May shifted in the rocking chair, trying to get comfortable. Her lower back was aching deep inside, and her ankles were swollen.

She thought her face looked puffy this morning, too. Just what she needed—extra bloating to add to her plumpness. She didn't want to tell the doctor that her urine was unusually dark and low in quantity, but she guessed she'd have to, since her health was falling off. He would probably tell her to take warm baths again. As if she had time to loll around in a bath!

May adjusted her spectacles on her nose. Now that she and Al were almost fifty, they both needed eyeglasses for close-up work. She thumbed carefully through the scrapbook pages. Here it was: the wording she needed. Taking her fountain pen, she jotted a few paragraphs into today's speech notes. While she wrote, she could hear workmen tromping around on the roof, getting ready to add three more stories to the Hutton Building.

Between today's appointments, she would send a baby gift to Gus and Myrtle for their brand-new daughter. It would be nice when the Paulsens' office building was complete so the two couples could resume their neighborly camaraderie. May liked Myrtle's sweet nature and the fact that she had a lot of charitable plans up her sleeve, especially for the Red Cross.

There were a few dreadful drawbacks to being wealthy. May didn't know how Gus and Myrtle had endured that terrible plot to kidnap their children for ransom. Gus had found out about the scheme and prevented the whole thing. Still, she imagined it made them nervous, especially while their little ones were so young and vulnerable.

If there was time this week, she wanted to visit Elizabeth, too. She chuckled to herself. It hadn't taken much effort to match Elizabeth, a pretty young mother from the Florence Crittenton Home, with that nice rancher. May wanted to make sure Elizabeth was happy and her baby girl was thriving. If only all of her efforts brought such good results. That handsome young man was honest and hardworking. He didn't mind a bit that his wife was a "fallen" woman who brought with her another man's baby. He just wanted companionship and love. Elizabeth offered those in abundance. They had married, right here in the Hutton living room, a few months after May introduced them.

She dressed carefully, took her speech notes from the table, and made her way downstairs. She'd stop at Davenport's Restaurant for a cup of coffee and one of their buttery bakery rolls first. Maybe that would make her head quit pounding and take away some of the pain in her back.

CHAPTER 49

Al Hutton – December 1910

He sat in his wood-paneled office and listened to the sounds coming from the spacious drawing room on the other side of the wall. May was hosting a celebration party to mark the success of the suffrage movement. A week ago, Washington women gained the right to vote, thanks in large part to May's steady work. She had labored long and hard for this victory. It hadn't come easily. This time, she had endured rejection and resistance from some of the other suffrage leaders. It hadn't fazed her, though. She reacted by stepping up her efforts and campaigning harder and more independently than ever before.

Music from a small orchestra and the din of several hundred voices, mostly female, came through the wall. He could smell fresh coffee, pastries, and perfume. In a few minutes, he would join the group, congratulate them, and then slip away to the lodge.

Taking a last puff on his pipe, he went to the window and looked out. Already it was dark, although it was barely five o'clock, and snow fell softly. He liked the way it covered the dirty streets below and softened the streetlights. In fact, he liked Spokane in general. He'd been thinking about building May a spacious house that overlooked the city just beneath those basalt cliffs to the south. One of these days, he'd ask her about it.

He returned to his desk and reread the letter he had just received from Harry. The Hercules was going strong, his friend reported. The long court case against the trust company was promising, although it was not completely settled yet. The lead-silver ore kept getting more abundant; in fact, the Hercules was now the third most profitable mine in the Coeur d'Alene district. Some people were calling it the Mighty Hercules.

He was glad that scoundrel Harry Orchard had sold his share of the Hercules when he did. He was in jail now, convicted of assassinating Idaho's governor. Clarence Darrow and William Borah had become famous in the trial of the men Orchard tried to implicate. The convict was said to be a model prisoner, but his shenanigans had wreaked havoc in Idaho. Some people said he was part of that awful plot to kidnap Gus's children.

Wallace was a mess these days. The gigantic forest fire that burned up three million acres across Idaho and Montana last summer had done dreadful damage there. This time the downtown had mostly been spared, thanks to all those brick buildings, but whole blocks of wooden structures and homes were gone. A few people had been killed. He made a mental note to take another trip over there and see who needed help.

He adjusted his shirt collar and made his way to the living room, pausing at the door to size up the crowd. They were all here, those suffragettes. He had to hand it to them. Despite their disagreement about tactics, they had convinced a bunch of powerful men that women should vote. The ballot measure to amend the Washington State Constitution had passed by a margin of almost two to one. Only four other states had accomplished the same feat.

The suffragettes were absolutely right. A ballot cast by a woman like May showed political understanding and intelligence, and he'd met a lot of others like her.

He made his rounds of the room, greeting and congratulating them. After a while, he managed to plant himself by the buffet table and help himself to a couple of fancy desserts.

May always said that one of the happiest days of her life was when she gained the right to vote in Idaho. Now, here she was for a second time. He glanced across the room and watched her throw back her head and roar with laughter. She was in her element today, decked out in an emerald satin dress and surrounded by important people.

He worried about May, though. Between her community projects, committee meetings, and charitable activities, she was exhausted. Even in her leisure time, she was forever writing letters to such people as John D. Rockefeller or William Borah about political issues. He wished she'd rest more. When Lyman had suggested the same thing, she'd written back and told him she would rest when she could see nothing more to do for humanity. That was May for you. That was another thing he loved about her.

He slipped from the room and headed downstairs. The lodge would be dark and quiet this time of day and he could read the *Spokesman Review* or play a game of cards while he sipped his coffee.

He had his own big plans for humanity. Someday, he wanted to build a comfortable home for orphaned children, safe from the world's harshness. Both he and May knew what it was like to be an orphan. How well he remembered the long, dark days after his parents died—days of too little affection and so much hard work that he'd had to quit school.

Maybe it was time to start thinking about making his dream come true.

CHAPTER 50

August 1911

May paused in the shade of a bushy alder and looked out over the glinting river. Flowing water always soothed her, and boy, did she need soothing this afternoon. Normally when she was riled up, she felt a surge of strength, but today she was tired and heavyhearted. Here was the perfect place to be alone: a cool, grassy spot beside the swift current of the Spokane River.

Her knees and back ached as she settled herself on the ground, took off her plumed hat, and pulled her long summer skirt to mid-thigh to cool off. Aching knees, she figured, was just old age creeping up. After all, she was fifty-one years old. Her hair, loosely pulled back in a soft puff that framed her face, was turning gray at the temples. She and Al joked that their combined ages added up to more than a century.

That other problem, though, was something bigger. It was the reason she didn't want to go home yet. The doctor had upset her just now with his frank talk about what ailed her. He said May's kidneys were the problem. If so, they sure did affect her whole body with headaches, backaches, and fatigue. Today he'd pointed out that her ankles were swollen again. She took off her shoes and stockings and scooted closer to the water, dipping her feet and legs into the stream. The current tugged on them, as if trying to pull her into its gentle flow.

The doctor had spoken kindly when he told her she had the early symptoms of Bright's disease, a chronic kidney malady. The illness would progress, he said. She had leaned forward in his black leather patient's chair and pressed him for information. He tried to soften the news by listing the things she could do to help. Jotting some notes for her as he talked, he instructed her to avoid getting cold or tired. She wasn't to lift heavy loads or let herself get emotionally exhausted. He mentioned mineral baths again. Baths did make her feel better, even if they didn't cure anything. And he said she should avoid meat in her diet. That was an unpleasant thought. No more crisp fried chicken or her favorite pot roast.

Once, a couple of years ago when she and Al were in San Francisco, Al had taken her to a leading physician there, who also suggested she might be developing kidney disease. May wasn't one to mope around feeling sorry for herself. Still, there was no cure for Bright's disease. The best she could do was control the symptoms.

She dipped her legs deeper into the river. Some days now she found it hard to work, but she made up for them by exerting herself in between. Nothing was going to get in the way of her projects, especially the ones making a difference in people's lives.

She knew what Al's response would be to today's news. He would sit with her, nodding and holding her hand. Then he might take her for a restful drive in the Flyer and suggest dinner at Davenport's Restaurant. And he would vow to help. They would find the best doctors and treatment money could buy. Tomorrow he would start looking into it.

She didn't want to think about what would happen if their efforts were unsuccessful.

The hem of her skirt fell into the water, and she left it there. Overhead, the dark-green leaves rustled in a soft breeze. A patch of sunlight fell on her cheek. She lifted her face and closed her eyes. Al would be well cared for, no matter what. There were plenty of people to cook and clean and drive for him. It wasn't that. It was his happiness that worried her. She and Al were like peas in a pod. The thought of him living alone made the lump in her throat grow bigger. That was another thing she would put out of her mind today.

She took a deep breath. With her eyes shut, she pictured herself back in Idaho, sitting beside the South Fork of the Coeur d'Alene, inhaling the same musty fragrances and listening to the same musical rippling sounds. As long as she didn't look, she couldn't see that the mountains were missing. The Spokane Valley had a different beauty: It was broad and gentle, interspersed with black basalt boulders and sheer rock faces. There were hills that people called mountains, but they weren't—not by Idaho standards. Without those steep slopes looming over her, May felt exposed somehow, as if mountains offered a protective presence. She lay back on the grass, shielding her eyes with her arm.

When she awoke, the sun was sliding toward the western horizon. Al would be wondering where she was. Still, she rested quietly for a few more minutes, gathering the energy to get up.

The key to living with Bright's disease, she supposed, was just that. Live. Make every day count.

She sat up and straightened her back. The disease might require that she rest more often, but, damn it, she would charge full steam ahead! The coming month was critical to helping California women get the vote. There were other events calling for her attention, too: deadly mine explosions, rumors of conflict brewing in Europe, suffragists across the country gearing up for a national crusade. The thought gave her the energy to push to her feet.

She pulled her soaked hem from the river, wrung out the fabric, and used it to dry her pale legs. The cold water had done wonders for the swelling. Thrusting her bare feet into her shoes, she stuffed her stockings in her pocket and began the short walk home. Bright's disease or not, she had work to do.

CHAPTER 51

Al Hutton – August 1911

He climbed the Carnegie Library's steps, passed between its grand columns, and pulled open the massive door. A rush of cool air greeted him. His footsteps echoed on the marble floor as he made his way to the circulation desk. Nearby, a clock ticked loudly. He stopped at the counter, where a woman with wavy brown hair and a nameplate that read "Miss Maxwell" looked up from her work.

"May I help you, sir?"

"Yes, please. I'd like some information about Bright's disease." He swallowed. "Nothing too technical."

"Right away, sir. If you wouldn't mind waiting a moment, I'll find what you need. Bright's disease—am I correct that it is a malady of the kidneys?"

"Yes." He couldn't get anything more past the constriction in his throat.

The librarian stood and walked to a side room, her graceful black skirt swishing in the silence. Her shoes must have had soft soles, because they didn't ring out like his own. He moved to a bench and gratefully sank onto it, closing his eyes for a moment. Images of last night flashed through his mind: May telling him what the doctor had said, the long drive beside the river, and dinner at Davenport's Restaurant, where he'd tried to act cheerful. Afterward, in bed, he'd reached out to stroke May's face and felt tears there.

The librarian's soft voice interrupted his thoughts. "Look over these books and see if they're what you need. If not, I can find you something more detailed." She studied his face. "Are you all right, sir?"

He stood up and took the heavy volumes from her. "Yes, yes, I'm fine, thank you. Now if you'll show me to your quietest room . . ."

She led him to a room with big windows overlooking the grounds. He chose a table in a shadowy corner. Sitting with his back to the room, he positioned his bifocal spectacles on his nose. This was one of those times when his lack of schooling would haunt him. Finding Bright's disease in this massive volume would be an ordeal. He began leafing through the pages.

A diagram of the human body caught his attention. There they were: the kidneys. Two small organs that, he now knew, could cause big problems. May's diagnosis explained something the two of them had laughed about since they'd lived in Wallace. Al had to make twice as many trips to the privy as May did. Today their private joke had become an ominous warning.

He glanced at his watch and began reading a section about kidneys. Maybe it would tell him exactly what was happening to May—although even the experts confessed there wasn't much known about Bright's disease. There might be tips for helping her feel better, though, or the names and locations of the best new doctors. He already knew where the finest mineral baths were. May had tried a lot of them by now.

That advice from the doctor about not getting exhausted, though— May was going to have to work on that. It wouldn't be easy. Her calendar's white pages were blue now, solidly covered with ink: scribbled dates for meetings, rallies, conventions, and little reminders about her charitable projects: "Deliver food basket to Children's Home," or "See Elizabeth at the ranch. Is the baby doing all right?" The dozens of places where May was to give speeches were jotted in capital letters. He couldn't fathom how she got it all done. She did, though, and still found time to host gatherings at the apartment or invite Josie to come from Wallace again for the weekend.

He took off his glasses and rubbed his eyes. Take today for example. May had been up and dressed before dawn to speak at a political breakfast. After that, she was going to the Florence Crittenton Home for a board meeting. There were two more meetings this afternoon, one involving the juvenile court and the other to advocate for female police matrons to oversee women jail inmates. Then, if he remembered right, she was delivering boxed dinners to the homeless men downtown. She said she'd be back for supper. Somehow she always had time to spend with him, like last Saturday when they'd driven to his favorite fishing hole on the St. Joe River.

He'd cancelled his own appointments today so he could be alone and think things through. Maybe he and May could hold this disease at bay. Thankfully, expense was no consideration. He would spend his last dime on treatments. Staring at the sunlight streaming in the library's windows, he thought about life without May. Instantly there was a hollow feeling in his chest and his throat closed. He rubbed his eyes again, shoved back his chair, and strode to the window. Despite the sun, the day seemed bleak, as if the brightness simply covered up a deeper gloom.

Sighing, he returned to his book and began reading again.

CHAPTER 52

Early Summer 1912

"You've found us a lovely spot, honey." May stood beneath the basalt cliffs southeast of downtown. "I can just imagine our house here, facing the valley."

"You like it? Me, too. We'll build it plenty big, with lots of bedrooms for guests. What do you think about a wide front porch with columns? We could sit outside and sip lemonade and remember when we were dirt poor." Al winked.

May smiled. "When we had to flounder through the snow to the privy."

"I'll buy the acreage this week if you're satisfied." Al brushed a bug off May's sleeve and gave her arm a little squeeze.

"I love it. Heck, it's a big chunk of property, but too much is better than not enough."

"Good. I'll make the arrangements."

May's mind whirled with the possibilities. The upstairs bedrooms would be large and airy with plenty of windows. A second-story balcony would hang out over the porch. Al could have his grand columns, and she would make sure there were enough fireplaces and a sweeping staircase. And, boy, did she have plans for the kitchen!

She would have to hire more help. Since her health problems began, she'd had to give up most of the household tasks and had hunted high and

179

low for a cook who could manage frequent large luncheons and dinner parties. She had also hired Belle, her stenographer, who was becoming more a friend than just a typist. Al had a driver along with the workmen and deliverymen who helped maintain the Hutton Building.

As the car coasted down the hill to town, May reminded herself that she had more important goals than building a house. Now that California's suffrage proposition had passed, she was throwing her support behind the movement in Oregon. And the Democratic National Convention was coming up soon in Baltimore. She would attend that, come hell or high water.

There were a thousand things to do before she left.

"Al, could we stop by the Regal on the way home?" She and Al owned the Regal Shoe Store now. "I met a family the other day with the sweetest mother who's working day and night to support her children. Six of them, all boys. Not one of them has a decent pair of shoes. They just can't afford them. I've got their sizes. Let's pick out a pair for each of them and send them out to their house."

Al reached over and took her hand. "Have you ever wondered how many folks you've helped through the years? All those Thanksgiving turkeys you've delivered, all the envelopes you've slipped to people on the streets? Even the women locked up in the jail have you to thank for better conditions. The kids over at the Children's Home think you're an angel. And those girls at the Crittenton Home? They love you like a mother."

"Oh, honey, you give me too much credit."

"No, I mean it. You're the biggest-hearted, most generous person I know. Plus, you get things done. A lot of people have good intentions but never take action."

❧

The heat here in Baltimore was stifling. This hotel was a fancy affair, but her room was humid and hot. May put the key on her bedside table and fanned herself with her limp gloves.

The National Democratic Convention had opened yesterday. It was a man's world here, but she was doing her utmost to change that. She was the first woman ever to attend from Washington State. Crossing the plush carpet to the upper-story window, she pulled aside the drapes and looked down. The Armory across the street was overflowing with male delegates dressed in formal black and white. Straw boater hats were perched on their heads like dinner plates. The men spilled onto the sidewalk and into the road. May wondered wryly if they were trying to get away from the choking cigar smoke inside. There were only a couple of ladies in the crowd. She wished it were different; there ought to be a few hundred women to show those men what was what.

Leaving the window, May slipped out of her long dress and filled her basin with cool water to wash her hands and face. She'd better mind herself and not overdo it so she wouldn't have another attack of Bright's disease—including high fever and unbearable retching—so far from home. With the washcloth, she wet her hot arms and neck, and then rinsed out her extra undergarments. In this humidity, they would take forever to dry. Maybe it was possible to hang them outside her window to catch the breeze. If the management complained, too bad. She needed her corset for tomorrow.

There was plenty of time to dress for dinner. May sat on the edge of the bed, absently running her fingers over its brown velvet spread. She'd wear the cream-colored gown with its lacy bodice and her new hat festooned with soft black plumes. First, though, she'd better send Al a note. He'd be wondering about her. She made a mental note to buy a souvenir for him. Baltimore had better shopping than Spokane. There wouldn't be much time for visiting stores, but the shops in the hotel lobby glittered with fancy gifts. Maybe he'd like some gold cuff links. Taking a sheet of hotel stationery from the bedside table, she found her pen.

Hi honey,

I'll write more when I can, but I just wanted to let you know that I arrived in Baltimore just fine. The train ride was far too long, but comfortable. Those Pullman sleeping cars are wonderful. The porters are so friendly and helpful—they see to your every need, even making up your berth when it's time. And the dining car is exceptional. There are fresh flowers in silver bud vases on the tables and finger bowls to use after your meal. I had a big baked apple drowned in cream for breakfast one day, and it was the best I've ever tasted.

The convention started yesterday. I'm drowning in a sea of men, but it doesn't bother me any. In fact, it makes me more determined to make myself heard. I'm planning to speak at every opportunity.

I'm taking good care of my health, so you can stop worrying. There's time for a quick nap before dinner. I want to have plenty of energy tonight. There will be a lot of powerful people to brush elbows with, all clustered in the gilded hotel dining room downstairs. I don't want to miss a minute.

Sending my love across the distance! I'll be home before you know it.

May

CHAPTER 53

November 1914

THE HOUSE WAS DONE.

The word "house" didn't begin to describe the elegance of their stately new home. "Mansion" seemed more fitting, but Al said that was pretentious.

The three-story white structure sat back from the street. Ten Tuscan columns defined the front, along with a full-length veranda, just as they had planned. Above the porch were second-floor and third-floor balconies, each with ornamental railings. May and Al could sit on the veranda enjoying the view of the city and the Spokane Valley summer or winter, since one of their three fireplaces—a redbrick one—was built out there, facing the porch from the outer surface of the house. New trees and a sprawling lawn contained by a low rock wall set the house apart from the woods and the cliffs that rose behind them. There was a curving driveway that led to the portico, the garage, and the cozy chauffeur's quarters. The park they had donated to the city was just beyond the stone wall.

The house's interior—all five thousand square feet of it—was a masterpiece, if May did say so herself. She loved the elegant entry hall and the grand staircase leading to the sunny bedrooms above. There were all the newest conveniences: an electric cooking range, a modern laundry, a sewing room, and even concealed radiators. Gleaming mahogany woodwork offset the glass doorknobs and rich embossed wallpaper. Along with the vast living room and formal dining room, the house had a basement and an attic, as well as an attached greenhouse. The streetcar line ended nearby, which meant that friends who had neither a carriage nor an automobile could visit.

May had made sure that for every dollar she and Al spent on their new home, they gave even more to charity. The dividends from the Hercules kept pouring in so fast that she never had to think about expense.

She leaned back in her rocker and sighed with happiness. There was nothing she lacked, except, of course, her health. Al had even built her a little log cabin out back where she could do her writing in peace and quiet. He'd wanted something to remind them of their first home, high on the mountainside above Wallace.

Al came through the door, carrying an armload of firewood, and threw another log on the flames. The house was heated by coal-fired hot water, but Al liked fireplaces. He settled into the matching rocker beside her.

"How are you feeling today?"

"Pretty good. I was sitting here feeling like a queen."

"Good. You deserve it."

They sat in companionable silence for a few minutes, watching the flames. Then May turned to him. "I sure hope Woodrow Wilson will keep his head about him. I can't bear the thought of this country getting involved in that awful war in Europe."

"I had lunch with Gus today at the Chamber of Commerce," Al answered. "He thinks we'll get into it sooner or later."

"We can't let that happen. I've got to do something. Look at what Jeannette Rankin is getting done in Montana for suffrage and world peace. Maybe I'll start a peace movement here."

"You could do it if anyone can, May. But you've got to stop taking on such big projects."

"I could manage it. With all this household help, I hardly have to lift a finger here at home."

They rocked quietly for a few minutes. Al studied her silhouette, then leaned forward. "I'd like to have your portrait taken, May. You look so pretty sitting there in the firelight."

"Thank you, honey."

"Too bad Nellie Stockbridge isn't closer. I love the way she takes photographs."

"Me, too. She's a real artist. Maybe we can sit for a portrait together. I'll look more slender, for once in my life. I've lost a lot of weight with this illness."

"I love you whatever your weight. But I want this photograph to be just of you."

Al was the world's best husband. She leaned over and reached for his hand. Whatever happened down the road, she had Al. She always had Al.

CHAPTER 54

Al Hutton – Spring 1915

It didn't look as though May was going to get better.

He puttered in the garden trimming the flowers, a job he did himself despite having the gardener. It gave a person time to think.

More and more often, she endured those attacks of fever, pain, and vomiting. They had tried everything that might help. The big-name doctors he brought in examined her thoroughly. Every one of them had ideas about what to do. But the fact was, Bright's disease was incurable. They had all told him so. He swallowed and looked up at the sky, his eyes following a flock of geese winging their way north.

He stayed by her side when she had her attacks. The most recent one had been the worst yet. He could at least hold her hand, even if watching her suffer made him agonize with helplessness. Sometimes he would gently wash her face, if the nurse was busy, or read to her. When she finally got strong enough, they took drives in the sunshine, rested on the porch, or just enjoyed their quiet meals together.

For once in her life, May was up against an obstacle too big for her. Still, she made good use of the time she was laid up. Sometimes when he came in from a trip downtown, she would be propped up in bed with the windows open wide and the sunshine pouring in. The stenographer would be sitting beside the bed, scribbling at high speed while May dictated a political opinion, a letter to the editor, or a humorous note to a friend. He had made dozens of trips to the post office to mail them for her.

What impressed him was that no matter how sick she was, May never lost sight of her goals. She still managed to make life better for others. Only last week, she had asked him to deliver another carload of clothing to the Spokane Children's Home, where the whole brood had gone wild over the brand-new pants and pretty dresses. May wasn't about to forget the Huttons' commitment to the Children's Home just because she had to be holed up at home.

He snipped off a bright yellow daffodil and trimmed the stem. A bouquet of these would look nice on May's windowsill.

Today he'd contact the Christian Science practitioner she had asked about. May sure was open to new ideas. Back in Wallace, she had chosen the Episcopal Church, mainly because she liked the bishop. Here in Spokane, she belonged to the Methodist Church. It seemed to him that May's religion was like the rest of her: all encompassing and broad-minded. She had devotion in abundance, and the good Lord knew she practiced faith through good works. But she didn't subscribe to just one hard-and-fast religion. May could see the good in all denominations. Maybe a practitioner could be of some help.

A streetcar pulled up to its stop, and its doors opened. A woman and six children clambered off. The youngsters made a beeline for the park while the woman, probably their mother, strolled behind, carrying a big wicker picnic basket. As he watched, the children began a noisy game of tag, chasing each other across the grass and dashing between the big ponderosa pine trunks.

Children. How he and May loved them. Too bad it hadn't worked out for them to have a family. He still yearned to have little ones around. Like May, he really felt for kids who didn't have parents to love and protect them. An idea that had been forming in his mind for months was starting to take shape. Why not build his orphanage right here in Spokane?

It wouldn't be a big, cold institution, like so many children's homes. Instead, he pictured a cluster of brick cottages surrounded by trees and grass, each one like a comfortable home overseen by a devoted housemother. There would be plenty of space where the children could run and play—and yes, work, because that would anchor them and make them strong. He would find a spread of land, with a sledding hill and space for a ball field and . . . Just thinking about it lifted his spirits.

He picked more daffodils and started for the kitchen.

CHAPTER 55

Summer 1915

MAY SAT ON THE VERANDA IN HER FLOWING WHITE GOWN, LOOKING OUT over the gently sloping grounds. This wheelchair sure was uncomfortable, despite the pillows Al had arranged on the wooden seat for her. It was heavy, too. She still had enough strength in her arms to move it, though.

Nearly a thousand Women's Club members stood in small groups around the house, talking and eating dainty sandwiches. Others sat in lawn chairs, balancing china plates on their laps. They looked like a bouquet of flowers in their long pastel dresses. A few used parasols to keep the summer sun off their faces. Off to the side, a small orchestra with a piano played a Mozart concerto.

Eliza darted from the house balancing a tray with tall glasses of lemonade. A few minutes later, she brought a plate of croissants and another of shortbread cookies.

Suspended from the white balcony railing above May's head, a banner fluttered in the afternoon breeze. It said SPOKANE WOMEN FOR WORLD PEACE.

Her old friend, William Jennings Bryan, would approve. He was now Secretary of State under President Wilson and had been here visiting recently. May had been recuperating from a bad bout when he traveled through Spokane stumping for peace, so he had come to the house to see her. She hadn't been full of her usual vim and vigor, but they'd had a nice talk. In her opinion, he was a better man than either Roosevelt or Taft. Too bad he never became president. Maybe there was still time for that in the future.

She had wanted to take him to see the Liberty Theater but hadn't been well enough to leave the house. The theater was the newest of Al's investments downtown, and it was something to see. On opening night, she and Al had sat in their box seats, dressed to kill, overlooking the gilded interior and nearly all of Spokane's upper-crust society. It had struck her as symbolic to be looking down on the self-important folks who still sometimes looked down on her. Although she had learned to temper her tongue a little, her colorful language and lack of formal schooling didn't fit in any better here than it had in Wallace. It didn't bother her anymore. Heck, her self-taught knowledge surpassed any college education. She could write flawlessly and her vocabulary was, if she did say so, extensive. She no longer cared if people recoiled from her strong opinions. It pleased her that she was too honest to be anything but blunt. Most folks liked her, and she had friends from all walks of life.

Her peace poem, "The Song of the Soldier Boy," had been set to music and was now sung at all the Liberty's evening performances. Proceeds from its sale went to charity.

She felt better today than she had in a long time. Her most recent attack of Bright's disease had been so severe that she wasn't sure she would ever recover. Once her legs were stronger, she would begin walking again. Already she could ride downtown in the new Pierce Arrow with Bert, their chauffeur. She and Al had gone to Hot Springs, Montana, to try the natural baths there. The mineral water did seem to help. And Al, of course, had called in every doctor, nurse, healer, and practitioner he could find.

Eliza darted by again, and this time May stopped her. With a wink, she took a little huckleberry tart—made from the old diner recipe—from Eliza's tray and popped it into her mouth. For an instant, the buttery pastry and sweet fruit took her back to the Silver Valley where, in her fruit-stained overalls, she had climbed the mountain slopes picking juicy berries—and then baked them into mouthwatering tarts for a certain handsome train engineer.

Her quiet moment was over. A cluster of ladies had spotted her sitting on the veranda. They were heading in her direction.

"May, what a beautiful gown!" one of them called out, her glance avoiding May's wheelchair.

"It sure beats the overalls I used to wear at the mine." May winked. "Come on over here, ladies. I have something to say."

The crowd gathered on the lawn beneath the veranda, filling the afternoon with the rustling of skirts and the fragrance of mingled perfumes.

May wheeled herself to the railing and pulled herself to her feet. She held up her hands as she stood facing the crowd. It was a few moments before they quieted and she was able to speak.

"Thank you all for coming. The Spokane Women for World Peace welcome you. There's a petition for you all to sign inside on the table, thanking President Wilson for keeping the United States out of the war in Europe. Please take time to add your signature. We'll send it to him immediately. He needs to know that there are plenty of us out here who support peace."

As the crowd cheered, May sank back into her chair, pale and exhausted. Beside her, the president of the Washington State Federation of Women's Clubs stepped to the railing and the crowd quieted again.

"We would like to thank Mrs. Hutton for inviting us to her beautiful estate today. I'm sure all of you know of her efforts to promote world peace, but some of you might not be familiar with her activities elsewhere, especially with the Democratic Party. She has also labored tirelessly for workers' rights, the Spokane Children's Home, the Florence Crittenton Home, and the city's Charities Commission. The women of Washington State can now vote, thanks in great part to her work for suffrage. Beyond those organized activities, Mrs. Hutton has spent thousands of dollars and countless hours doing good deeds for the lonely, the ill, and the destitute. There's been no publicity about her kindness to children, the baskets of food she has delivered, or the countless pairs of shoes she has given away. The men on skid row could tell you a few nice things about her, too." She turned and faced May. "Thank you, Mrs. Hutton, for all you have done for Spokane and its surroundings. And thank you for your hospitality on this beautiful summer day."

Amid a roar of applause, May spotted Al out on the lawn, beaming. Those words were like a melody to her. She had hitched her wagon to a star, all right, and had done her best to shine. There was still plenty of work to be done. But today, she would simply enjoy this grand gathering.

Sunshine fell across her lap, warming her. In the sweet-scented park beyond the rock wall, children splashed in the wading pool Al had dedicated in her honor. He stood in the leafy shade, clapping loud and long after the others had stopped. She met his eyes across the sea of faces, blew him a kiss, and then wheeled herself inside to be the first to sign the petition.

Epilogue

On October 6, 1915, May Arkwright Hutton died at home with Al by her side. Her death was announced in newspapers from San Francisco to New York.

Hundreds of people gathered at the Hutton home, where the funeral was held. Extra streetcars were required to bring the throng, and private automobiles lined the nearby streets. The crowd spilled out of the sprawling house into the yard and driveway.

In the crowd were teary-eyed young women holding onto toddlers. There were eminent politicians and businessmen in black coats and starched collars, standing side by side with miners wearing tattered canvas work pants. College-educated suffragists brushed elbows with laundresses and cooks. Proper club women mixed with red-light girls. Elderly women leaning on canes struggled to stand tall in tribute, and freckled children asked in hushed voices where Auntie May had gone. Coming from near and far, they were as diverse as May's life itself. Each had a personal connection to the woman they honored.

To many, she was a generous benefactor, or a witty friend who lived by her own counsel. To others, she was a courageous and devoted sister for suffrage. Some saw her as a great-hearted humanitarian, while others remembered her as a down-to-earth diner cook with a free tongue. To Al, she was a beloved life partner and best friend.

It was difficult for Al to carry on without her, but within a year after her death, he purchased a large piece of property nestled on the beautiful north flank of the Spokane Valley. In honor of May, he built and endowed the Hutton Settlement, a home for orphaned and needy children. Al spared no expense in creating a cluster of homey brick cottages where youngsters could thrive and grow, nurtured in a stable environment. The community also included a gymnasium, a barn, and acres of farmland. Al poured his heart into the project, ensuring the Settlement's success. He built it, he said, to last at least 250 years.

Al oversaw the establishment, where he was a frequent visitor until his death in 1928. Photos from the 1920s show him surrounded by the children he loved and provided for, many of whom called him "Daddy Hutton." In one picture, his hands rest lightly on the shoulders of the smallest tousled boy. Al had finally found his sons and daughters.

Today, the Hutton Settlement is still in full operation. The campus is now 319 acres, and the decades have brought the additions of a swimming pool, a playground, and a Christmas tree farm. But the solid principles upon which the home was founded remain the same.

Al and May Arkwright Hutton are still a presence at the Settlement. Photographs and tributes bring them to mind, and their endowment plays a continued critical role. The extraordinary philanthropists—once a simple locomotive engineer and a rough-edged diner cook—will never be forgotten by the thousands of children who have found a warm haven there.

Evidence of May and Al lingers in downtown Spokane, too, where the massive Hutton Building sprawls along an entire city block. Other structures that once felt the couple's presence and influence also remain, including their imposing Spokane home, which is still a private residence.

Meandering up Canyon Creek from Wallace, Idaho, one can see remnants of old mines and mining settlements like Burke. In the town of Wallace, the Huttons' tall, narrow Pine Street house sits proudly in a quiet residential district, well tended by its present owners. Many of the buildings where the Huttons did business and attended social events have been preserved, because every downtown building in Wallace is listed on the National Register of Historical Places.

Those interested in learning more about the Huttons' lives can explore the May Arkwright Hutton Papers held by the Eastern Washington State Historical Society/Northwest Museum of Arts & Culture. Researchers there can view photographs, letters, and other items, including May's scrapbooks, in the Joel E. Ferris Research Library and Archives, or study the museum's online collection. Many resources are available through the online Washington Women's History Consortium. Books and articles published through the years are readily accessible at public libraries. Also, the University of Idaho holds the incredible Barnard-Stockbridge Photograph Collection documenting Wallace's history. Nellie Stockbridge would be astounded to see hundreds of her beautiful black-and-white images housed in the library and in digital form online.

May Arkwright Hutton once wrote to her half-brother: "Now Lyman, you just watch my smoke, because I am going to do things." Despite her lighthearted tone, those words summarized May's approach to life. By making a beeline toward her dreams, and using her passionate beliefs as a compass, she made enormous strides for humanity during her lifetime. Together with her beloved Al, she had an enduring impact on the Inland Northwest and those who live there.

Al Hutton (seated at center) with children at the Hutton Settlement Christmas party, 1921

Taken by buildings at Hercules No. 2 level. L to R: Ed Hedin, a Day employee; Emma Markwell; Henry Floyd Samuels; May Hutton; Jerome Day; Miss Hedin (sister of Ed Hedin); Myrtle White (who married Paulsen), and L. W. Hutton, wearing a cook's apron. August Paulsen stands on the wood pile.

May Arkwright Hutton (seated, fourth from left), Al Hutton (standing at right), and others at the Hercules Mine

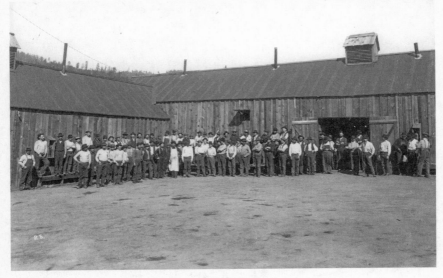

A group picture of miners in the bull pen, 1899

Left to Right: May Hutton; Emma Markwell; Miss Hedin, sister of Ed Hedin; Ed Hedin; L. W. Hutton; August Paulsen; Myrtle White, who married Paulsen; and Henry Floyd Samuels.

Hercules Mine: group examining ore samples by candlelight. May Arkwright Hutton is first on the left; Al Hutton is in the center.

May Hutton, near the end of her life

Acknowledgments

MANY HEARTFELT THANKS TO THE GENEROUS PEOPLE WHO HELPED SEE this book to completion.

I am especially indebted to May Arkwright Hutton and Levi W. (Al) Hutton, the pioneers who inspired this story with their altruistic responses to personal life events, and to the other historical men and women who appear in these pages, especially early photographers Nellie Stockbridge and T. N. Barnard.

My deep gratitude also belongs to those who:

- explored the streets of Wallace, Idaho, with me and drove those many slow miles on the winding back roads to Murray and Burke.

- helped me search Spokane, Washington, to find the Huttons' downtown drawing room, the imposing Paulsen Building, May and Al's elegant tree-shaded residence, the remarkable Hutton Settlement, and more.

- wielded the world's best critiquing pen and spent months offering solid writing suggestions (thanks, and more thanks, to fellow author Maggie Plummer).

- shared colorful interpretations of May Arkwright Hutton from their own personal research.

- provided hearty opinions about May—and helped me learn and appreciate the intricate history of the Silver Valley.

- obtained hard-to-find research materials and showed interest in this project from the start (my friends and coworkers at North Lake County Public Library, Polson, Montana).

- gave me white gloves and guided me through the adventure of browsing May's archived scrapbooks, letters, and photos at Spokane's Joel E. Ferris Research Library and Archives (Northwest Museum of Arts & Culture).

- answered questions about silver mining, life in a mining town, railroading, suffrage, cooking on a woodstove, Bright's disease, the Hutton Settlement, and countless other aspects of this story.

- read manuscript drafts and gave timely and insightful suggestions.

- filled in for me when I occasionally needed time off from work or everyday commitments to write.

- offered continual words of encouragement and support.

- wrote and published earlier books, articles, maps, descriptions, etc., about the Huttons and early Idaho/Washington history, or created websites and access to digital photographs that made my work easier and more complete.

- gave ongoing editorial advice, immediate answers to my questions, and helpful support from afar (my gratitude to Erin Turner).

- expertly turned a manuscript into a finished book—with all the hard work and skill that the process involves (the dedicated folks at Globe Pequot Press).

Thank you all.

About the Author

Mary Barmeyer O'Brien was born and raised in Missoula, Montana, and received her BA from Linfield College in McMinnville, Oregon. She is the author of seven books, including several nonfiction accounts of pioneers on the overland trails and three western historical novels based on the lives of real pioneer women. Mary works at her local public library and writes from her home in Polson, Montana. She and her husband, Dan, a high school science teacher, have three grown children.